D1530245

The Greatest Spy
Who Never Was

A HUGO DARE ADVENTURE

DAVID CODD

Dedicated to Helen, Olivia and Jack.

PROLOGUE

It's not easy being a spy.

I should know. Sometimes I can't even go deep undercover without being asked to do something I'd rather not. Like rob a bank. Or steal an antique statue. Still, rather that than be buried alive in a coffin. Or chased by a ferocious beast with a taste for human flesh.

Yes, like I said, it's not easy being a spy.

And yet, nothing could prepare me for what was about to happen next.

Against my better judgment, I was stood on the roof of a tall, three-storey building.

To make matters worse, there was a bitter chill in the night air, accompanied by a strong wind that was blowing a breeze straight up my pyjama bottoms.

And to cap it off, as if all that wasn't bad enough already, there was somebody behind me.

The *somebody* in question was pressing something long and sharp into the small of my back. No, not a sword. Not even a knife.

A knitting needle.

'*What are you waiting for, you revolting specimen? Jump!*'

That's me. The revolting specimen. Although you can call me Hugo. Hugo Dare. Because that's my name. It's on my birth certificate and everything. Thirteen years later and I'm on the cusp of greatness. SICK's newest recruit. The cream of Crooked Elbow. The king of the jungle. The cheese on the toast. The pea in the pod and the icing on the cake, all rolled into one. With a cherry on top.

And breathe …

Back on the roof, the wind changed direction and I caught a whiff of something unpleasant. It was the sour stench of greed.

Secrets of a Spy Number 56 – always judge a person by their smell.

'I thought I told you to jump!' hissed the *somebody* in my ear.

'There's no thinking about it,' I replied. 'You *did* tell me to jump. And I was about to. That is, until I had a thought of my own. I started to wonder what my brains would look like splattered all over the pavement. Baked beans at a guess. Mmm, delicious. Then I had another thought.'

'*Two thoughts in one day?*' smirked the somebody. 'I'm proud of you.'

'Don't be,' I said. 'It happens all the time. Well, *most* of the time … once in a while … okay, hardly ever, but let's not worry about that now. No, I've been trying to figure out the best way to make you pay for what you've done.'

'*Pay?*' the somebody sniggered. 'If only I'd brought some loose change.'

'Good joke,' I groaned, 'but only one person will be laughing when I get myself out of this particular fix ... and it won't be you!' I paused. 'It'll be me. And I *will* get out of it. Yes, I'm stood on the roof of a rather large building and yes, you want me to jump, but that doesn't mean anything. Not in the grand scheme of things. The way I see it, this isn't over 'til the fat lady— *whoa!*

My sentence was left hanging as I did the exact opposite. The *somebody* prodded, the knitting needle stabbed and my body jerked. I began to wobble. Then I did something else entirely.

I fell off the roof.

'Goodbye,' said the *somebody*. '*Forever.*'

This time there was no coming back. I was on my way. Over and out.

Going ... going ... gone.

1.'SPIES NEED THEIR PRIVACY.'

Let's hit the rewind button ...

My story starts one day, fifteen hours and twenty-one minutes before the events on the roof. Still, who's counting? Not me. I'm far too busy for that sort of nonsense. Besides, I don't have enough fingers. Or toes. Teeth maybe. Spots definitely, but there's no need to get personal. At least, not until we know each other a little better.

Allow me to set the scene. It was a Saturday in mid-winter. Morning. Early morning. Like ridiculously early, but then the life of spy is a twenty-four hours a day, seven days a week, a load more days in a month and a dozen or so months in a year occupation. I had no choice but to get on with it. So that was what I was doing now. Getting on with it. Albeit in a sluggish kind of way because I'd got out of bed far too early.

Breakfast – half a jar of pickled onions followed by a gulp of mouthwash – had been successfully seen off, leaving me free to get down to the real business of the day.

The business of laying down the law to some unscrupulous scoundrel.

'You're lower than a snake's belly!' I cried. 'More devious than a fish with feathers! Naughtier than a bull in a bungalow! There's only one place that you're going, monkey gums, and it's not to the dentist – *it's to prison!* The Crooked Clink to be precise, where all the rogues and wrong 'uns end up. Ah, you're all ears now, aren't you? Well, two ears and a particularly ugly face. If I had my way you'd be locked up, behind bars, from now until ... *the future*. Does that frighten you? Because it should do. Your toenails should be trembling like jelly on a roller coaster right about now. Mmm, gooseberry jelly. My favourite.'

I stopped mid-flow and slapped myself on the forehead. The last thing I wanted was to be distracted by even the mere mention of food.

'I sniffed you out a long time ago, bog-breath,' I said, tapping both nostrils to prove my point. 'In spying circles, I'm what's known as a big sniffer. Or is it just a bad smell? Either way, I've got a nose for crime.'

'Really, dear? I think you'll find you've got a nose for bogeys like most boys your age.'

I spun around, ready for anything. Unfortunately, *anything* turned out to be a tall, gangly woman with unnaturally frizzy hair and a bright orange housecoat. She smelled strongly of lavender, which made it even more astonishing that she had somehow managed to creep up on me unnoticed. She was also armed. Clutched in her right hand was what can only be described as a glass of milk. Because that was what it was. Obviously.

'Do you mind, Doreen?' I snapped. 'In future, please

knock before entering. Eight times should do the trick. Especially when I'm in the middle of grilling a particularly villainous villain.'

'*Grilling … a … villain?*' repeated Doreen slowly. 'There are no villains here, dear. Just a spade and a shovel. Plant pots and compost. Look around if you don't believe me. This is the garden shed. And you're all alone.'

'This is not just the garden shed, Doreen,' I argued. 'This is my bedroom.' That much was true. Aside from all the *gardeny* bits, I had my bed in there as well. 'We both know that I moved into the … *shedroom* so I wouldn't be disturbed. Spies need their privacy.'

'I wouldn't know about that … and neither would you, dear!' said Doreen, placing the glass of milk on the lawnmower (also known as my bedside table). 'You're not a spy,' she said bluntly. 'You're just a silly little schoolboy with an over-active imagination. And please don't call me Doreen.'

I flopped onto my bed in despair. 'That is your name, is it not?'

'It is, dear,' agreed Doreen, 'but I'm also your mother. Why don't you call me mummy like you used to?'

'*Mummy?*' I snorted. 'Dream on. I've got standards to uphold.'

'*Standards, dear?*' Doreen coughed twice. It was as close to laughter as she ever got. 'Like wearing bright yellow pyjamas with a matching dressing gown and slippers? Or just talking to yourself and your imaginary villain?'

Mother or not, I was getting nowhere with this woman. 'I'm practicing,' I explained. 'If I'm going to become a spy then the Chief of SICK needs to see that I'm the real deal.'

'Oh, dearie me, dear,' sighed Doreen. She pulled open the curtains to reveal a plastic window that was covered in cobwebs. 'You talk about as much sense as your father.'

'You mean Dirk Dare, the greatest spy who never was,' I said proudly.

'No, I mean Dirk Dare, the tea boy at the SICK Bucket,' frowned Doreen. 'Tea boy is only one tiny step up from toilet boy. He's the lowest of the low. The bottom of the heap. Do you know how happy that makes me feel?'

'Very,' I said.

'*Not* very, dear,' said Doreen sadly. 'If I'm being honest, your father has been a huge disappointment to me since the moment we met. He's nothing but a pork pie of a man.'

Now that was something I did agree with. 'You mean strong and meaty with a hard outer-casing?'

'No, I mean small and round and unnaturally crusty,' argued Doreen. 'And you'll go the same way if you're not careful. Your father may think getting you a weekend job at the SICK Bucket is in your best interests, but I don't agree. No; more homework is the way forward. I've begged Miss Stickler to give you extra, but she won't have it. Something tells me that your Headteacher doesn't like you very much. Well, *she* told me. With her own lips. She said you're like a wart she couldn't burn.'

'I didn't know that setting fire to students was still allowed these days,' I muttered under my breath. 'Listen, Doreen, school's not really the place for a highly skilled super spy like me. And, just so you know, highly skilled super spies don't drink milk either. Milk's for babies.'

'Of course it is, dear,' said Doreen. She ended the conversation with an obligatory roll of her eyes before turning to leave. If she wasn't my mother I'd have replaced her years ago. Still, contrary to what I'd just said, she did serve up a particularly refreshing glass of creamy, cow juice (although it was highly unlikely that she'd gone to the effort of squeezing the udder herself).

With my shedroom a Doreen-free zone, I was all set to take a sip when a curious sensation overwhelmed my entire body. For no apparent reason whatsoever, my armpit began to suddenly vibrate. Panic-stricken, I leapt to my feet, careful not to spill a single drop of milk as I got ready to hide behind the hedge trimmer.

Then the penny dropped.

Or rather, my mobile phone did.

Straight out the sleeve of my pyjamas and onto the shedroom floor. In hindsight, under my armpit probably wasn't the safest place to keep it. Although I'd still rather there than under someone else's armpit. That would just be unhygienic. Not to mention downright awkward whenever it rang.

I picked up my phone and answered on the sixth vibration. There was a slight delay before a muffled voice crackled into life.

'*Ugo Dayer?*'

It was a man. His accent was strong, but I couldn't quite place it. Certainly not from Crooked Elbow. Not even from the neighbouring town of Twisted Kneecap, but then they all speak as if they've got a vacuum cleaner strapped to their tonsils so I was hardly surprised.

'Ugo Dayer?' the caller repeated.

'Almost,' I said. 'It's actually Hugo Dare, but I won't hold it against you. Right, now we've cleared that up, fire away.'

The caller hesitated. 'Fire away?'

'Sure,' I said. 'Shoot.'

'*Shoot?*' The caller drew a breath. 'As you wish …'

Crack.

I blinked and my shedroom window shattered into one thousand and forty-three (approximately) tiny pieces of plastic.

Crack.

I blinked again and the glass I was holding exploded in my hand, showering me with milk.

I was about to blink for a third time but decided that the risk was too great. Instead, I dived back onto my bed, taking cover beneath my duvet. Like any thirteen-year-old boy under attack, I did what came naturally. Thankfully, my bladder was empty, so my next move was to check myself all over. As far as I could tell I was hole-free. I hadn't been hit. Now all I had to do was make sense of what was happening.

Call me paranoid, but it seemed that somebody was trying to kill me.

Call me stupid, but I had a feeling I'd just invited them to do it.

2. 'YOU COULD ALWAYS CALL ME MURDER!'

My fingernails were shaking as I pressed my phone to my ear.

'Do not be the shy boy, Ugo Dayer,' said the caller. 'Come out, come out, wherever you is.'

'No ... no ... not today, thank you,' I stammered. 'My mother always told me not to play with strange men. Or women. *Especially* not women. Besides, believe it or not, but some *serious screwball* just shot up my shedroom!'

'Oh, that I do believe,' said the caller, 'because I is that serious screwball!'

'*You!*' I shook my fist under the duvet until it dawned on me that the caller, my mystery sniper, couldn't see what I was doing. 'Well, that's not very nice, is it?' I said snottily.

'No, but then I is not a very nice person,' agreed the caller. 'I is mostly horrid.'

'At least you're honest,' I said, 'even if your manners are atrocious. Everyone knows it's bad etiquette to shoot at somebody without introducing yourself first. So, who is *I* exactly?'

The caller hesitated. 'My name is … Minkle Sparkes.'

'*Minkle Sparkes!*' It rang a bell, but not loud enough to drown out my laughter. 'You sound like a cheap firework!'

'You could always call me Murder,' said the caller. 'That is my professional title, after all … although I doubt you'll live long enough to remember it!'

I moved the phone away from my ear so I could gather my thoughts. The last thing I wanted was for Murder to live up to his name. And the only way I could avoid that was to conjure up a plan so fool proof that even a fool like me couldn't mess it up.

Luckily, I knew just the way to do it.

Secrets of a Spy Number 77 – if in doubt, stop thinking altogether.

It works. Trust me. Sure enough, the moment I switched off my brain, I had an idea. It all hinged on how much of me Murder could see. Yes, he knew I was in my shedroom, but did he have a proper view of inside? Because if he didn't, well, that meant I still had a slightly better than zero chance of getting out of there alive.

And *slightly better than zero* was good enough for me.

Mindful of the puddle of milk, not to mention the shards of broken glass that were bathing in it, I rolled out from under my duvet and dropped gently onto the wooden floor. Slowly, I began to slither towards the shedroom door. It was at this point that I realised Murder had gone worryingly quiet.

'You are still there, aren't you?' I asked.

I heard shuffling on the other end of the line. 'Apologies

are all mine,' Murder said eventually. 'I is currently unavailable.'

'*Currently unavailable?*' I shook my head in disgust, but then regretted it as my nose caught on a rusty nail that was sticking up from the floorboards. 'You've gone to all this effort to shoot me and then you get distracted,' I muttered. 'That's no way to behave.'

'I is just tying my shoelace,' Murder revealed. 'It is knotted. I may be some time.'

Murder's words were like a forty-piece orchestra to my eardrums. Suddenly I had a chance to get out of the shedroom and back to the house without being spotted. Then I would be safe. Well, *almost* safe. I still had my mother to contend with, and she would go bananas when she saw the shedroom window. Still, even Doreen would have to agree that shattered plastic was a small price to pay for my survival.

I think ...

With Murder temporarily out of action, I pushed the shedroom door to one side and set off across the back garden on my hands and knees. The sky was black, the grass was damp, and the neighbour's cat was unfriendly. When I reached the house, I yanked on the door handle and dived inside.

That was easier than I expected.

But it wasn't over yet.

Racing through the kitchen, I took to the stairs faster than a rat up a pair of skinny fit jeans. My destination was my old bedroom. Ever since I had moved outside, Doreen had been using it as a nursing home for sick and injured garden gnomes (don't ask; I'm embarrassed enough already). One gnome in particular was the focus of my attention. His name was Bertie. He had a red hat, a white beard and a broken wheelbarrow. Add to that a belly that was as wide as my head and he was perfect for what I had in mind.

I found Bertie laid out on a make-shift stretcher ready to be operated on. Scooping him up, I dodged another gnome – Errol – and made my way across the carpet. With my body hidden from view, I carefully opened the curtains, placed Bertie on the windowsill and looked between his legs.

Not only was Everyday Avenue a mundane, run-of-the-mill housing estate on the bland side of Crooked Elbow, it was also where I had called home since the day I was born. We lived at number thirteen. Unlucky for some perhaps, but up until then I had never found it to be so.

That all changed, however, when I shifted to one side and knelt on Errol's fishing rod.

'I is back,' announced Murder.

'Pleased to hear it,' I grumbled. 'You were gone so long I was starting to think you'd tied your tongue instead of your shoelace.'

I knew that Murder was close – as in close enough to shoot at me – but then how close was that? At first glance, everything outside looked completely normal. The trees and bushes were still and there was nothing out of the ordinary lurking in the shadows (ignoring, of course, the other eighty-seven gnomes that Doreen had lovingly collected in our front garden).

'So, Ugo Dayer, is I right in thinking that you refuse to come out of the shed?' said Murder.

'*Shedroom*,' I said, correcting him. I ducked my head and silently punched the air. My plan had worked. Murder couldn't see me. He had no idea I was in the house. 'But you are right about one thing,' I continued. 'I'm not coming out ... and there's nothing you can do about it!'

I looked beyond our front garden. There were several cars and a milk float parked up on the roadside, whilst every other house had their curtains closed and their lights out.

No. Wait. *Almost* every other house.

Number fourteen was the home of Mr and Mrs Simple. *Usually*.

This week they had gone camping in an active volcano (they always did like to holiday somewhere hot), meaning their house was empty. I knew this because Doreen had their door key. Her instructions were simple; much like the Simples themselves. Every day she had to feed the goldfish. And that was what puzzled me most.

How could a goldfish have turned on the lights and opened the curtains in the Simples' bedroom?

The answer came to me when a shadowy figure in a balaclava appeared in the window. This had nothing to do with fishy fingers.

Either the Simples were being burgled ... *or I had just found Murder.*

3.'MAYBE YOU IS NOT SO LUCKY ...'

Secrets of a Spy Number 82 – slowly, slowly, catchy criminal.

Or, in this case, *catchy* a balaclava-wearing bounder who had an unnatural dislike for yours truly. He didn't know it yet, but I practically had him in the palm of my hand. Well, *practically* practically. The way I saw it, he was only one small step away from a lengthy stretch in prison. Okay, several miles from the Crooked Clink, but let's not get bogged down in the detail.

With or without a rod, how hard could it be to reel him in? All I needed was some bait. Nothing too wriggly. Nothing that could fall off at the first nibble. And I knew just the thing.

Me.

'Listen, Murder.' My heart was fluttering like a butterfly on a treadmill as I began to speak. 'I know we've got off to a rocky start – some may even call it explosive – but it's not as if it can't be fixed. Why don't you pop round for a glass of milk and we can talk things over? Or, if you're feeling brave, a drop of the hard stuff. I've got a particularly strong mouthwash that I've been saving for a special occasion. One sip and you won't be able to feel your gums for weeks—'

'*Mouthwash?*' cried Murder. 'This is not the joke!'

'Do I look like I'm smiling?' I said, grinning to myself. My grin disappeared as Murder moved away from the Simple's window. Maybe he was leaving. And I couldn't let that happen. 'Don't go!' I said hastily. 'Not now we're such good friends.'

'You is the funny guy, Ugo Dayer,' said Murder, 'but you is also very foolish. This, I think, may be your downfall. Today you live, but tomorrow you may not be so lucky …'

Silence.

'Wait!' I shouted.

'What for?' said Murder.

'I don't know … I've not thought that far yet,' I mumbled. 'What about … Christmas? Or my birthday? No, *your* birthday? Ask nicely and I might even bake you a cake.'

'I is tired,' said Murder under his breath. 'Tired of *you*. Maybe I change my mind. Maybe you is not so lucky …'

The call ended abruptly. *Charming.* A moment later and Murder reappeared in the Simple's window. He had replaced his phone with something much longer and far more dangerous. Now I'm no expert on guns, but I know a gun when I see one.

And this was definitely a gun.

My stomach turned cartwheels as Murder pointed the barrel out of the window. Looking down the sight, he took aim and … *crack.*

Yes, I know that Murder was firing at my empty shedroom, but that still didn't stop me from diving beneath the window.

Crack ... crack ... crack.

Seven seconds later I raised my head and looked between Bertie's legs. The Simples' bedroom window had been closed and the curtains drawn. On the eighth second the light went out.

Murder was on his way.

And so was I.

I figured I had about one minute to get over to number fourteen before Murder disappeared for good. Like a coiled kangaroo, I sprang into action, bouncing towards the bedroom door as fast as my slippered feet would take me.

Which, as it happens, was too fast.

I blame Jasper. Up until then, he was a gnome who had been suffering from nothing more than a fractured arm. Now I had trod on him, however, he was no longer suffering at all (although he was in eleven separate pieces and impossible to repair).

Dropping to the floor, I pulled off my slipper and began to blow on my throbbing toes. Slowly, the pain began to fade.

A lot like my chances of catching Murder.

'Who's in there?'

I was about to call out when the door burst open, hitting me full in the face, knocking me backwards like a human domino.

'Oh, it's you—' Doreen pressed a hand to her mouth as

she caught sight of the unfortunate gnome. '*Jasper!*' she cried. 'You've been ... been ... been ... *flattened!*'

I tried to blank out the pain and concentrate on the time. If my calculations were correct, I had about thirty seconds left before Murder was gone. 'I'm going out,' I groaned, my head pounding as I climbed up off the carpet.

'You're still in your pyjamas,' said Doreen.

'A man called Murder just tried to shoot me and I don't want him to escape,' I explained.

'*Shoot you?* Of course he did,' sighed Doreen. 'And I suppose it was this Murder fellow who *murdered* Jasper as well, was it?'

'No, that was me,' I admitted. 'Although I'm not entirely sure it's possible to murder a garden gnome.'

I slipped back into my slippers and departed my old bedroom before my mother could argue. Out on the landing, I took to the stairs three at a time. Three steps later, the stairs took me. Still, at least I reached the bottom that little bit quicker.

Twenty seconds.

My eyes were trained on number fourteen as I hurried out of the house. I hit six more gnomes as I raced across the garden and dived over the hedge. I landed on my feet but stumbled forward.

Straight into the road.

Straight into a passing milk float.

4. 'NEVER HAVE LIKED MILKMEN.'

Ten seconds.

It was nothing more than a glancing blow, but the force of the milk float was still enough to knock me clean off my feet. As I lay there, flat on my stomach in the middle of the road, I had but one thought.

I could still catch Murder.

I looked up and tried to get my bearings. Number fourteen was straight in front of me. Or so I thought. It's hard to tell when your eyeballs are rattling about in their sockets.

Behind me, I heard the sound of *grinding* brakes as the milk float grumbled to a halt. It was followed by footsteps. I guessed it was the milkman coming to see if I was okay.

Digging my fingernails into the road, I dragged myself over the kerb and onto the pavement. I continued like this along the length of the Simples' driveway. I was getting closer to the door, but there was still no sign of Murder.

A foot on my shoulder was enough to stop me mid-drag. I shrugged it off and rolled onto my back, expecting to find the milkman stood behind me.

How wrong could I be?

All I could see was darkness. And two eyes peeking through the holes in a balaclava.

'You said I should pop round for a glass of the milk,' said Murder menacingly. 'Instead, I bring the milk to you. *Enjoy!*'

I watched in horror as he lifted an entire crate above his head. Now I like a glass of the cow's finest as much as anybody, but even I draw the line at having sixteen bottles, all full to the brim, dropped on me from a great height.

It was time for a course of drastic action.

A *crash* course.

Bending my back like a street-dancing eel, I lashed out with both feet, sending the crate flying out of Murder's hands. Aware that what goes up must always come down, I scrambled backwards until I collided with the Simples' garage door. As expected, the crate hit the concrete. Bottles exploded upon impact, sending jets of milk spurting into the air. I shielded my eyes and looked beyond the fountain of white stuff for Murder, but he was nowhere to be seen.

Then I spotted the milk float.

It was on the move; trundling towards the exit to Everyday Avenue. I pushed myself up, ready to give chase, but my legs refused and I collapsed in a sorry heap. When I looked again the milk float had gone.

Murder had escaped. And he had done so in the slowest getaway vehicle known to mankind.

'*Never have liked milkmen.*'

I jumped at the sound of a dull, monotone voice beside me. It belonged to a small, bedraggled man with a tangled mess of hair, lopsided spectacles and dark rings circling his eyes. He was dressed in a bright orange jacket that was covered in curious green stains and ripped shorts that had almost certainly started out as trousers. His shoes were so old that I guessed it was only the laces that were holding them together.

I didn't know his name, but I recognised him immediately.

It was the postman.

'That was no milkman,' I said. 'That was Murder.'

'*Murder?*' The postman shook his head. 'Is that what he told you? He should try doing my job! Been working all hours, I have. Midnight to midnight. Walked over two hundred miles … and that's just in the past three days. Been bitten by sixteen dogs … not to mention four cats … *and* a gerbil. Got stuck up a chimney. And trapped in a sewer. Still, better than being cooped up in the house I suppose.' The postman took a breath (and a break from complaining) as he removed an envelope from his bundle of mail. 'I've got a letter for a Master Hugo Dare,' he said.

Interesting. I didn't tend to receive much mail and even when I did it was only to take out insurance for the car I couldn't drive, or offer me new dentures to replace the teeth I hadn't lost yet.

'I am he,' I said, holding out my hand.

'I had a bad feeling you'd say that,' moaned the postman, as he passed me the envelope. 'Now, this letter is from somebody extremely high up.'

'Like at the top of a tree?' I asked. 'Or in a hot air balloon?'

'More like a position of power,' the postman revealed.

'No … it can't be … *not Miss Stickler!*' My teeth trembled at even the mere mention of the most formidable Headteacher ever to grace Crooked Comp'.

'No, not Miss Stickler,' said the postman, clearly irritated. 'Just open it and you'll find out.'

The envelope was handwritten in red. Blood perhaps. Or tomato sauce. Or, at a guess, red ink. That seemed the most logical explanation. It said:

> *Master Hugo Dare,*
> *Flat out on the Simples' driveway,*
> *14 Everyday Avenue,*
> *Crooked Elbow.*

I ripped the envelope apart before the excitement got the better of me. There was a single slip of paper inside. I read it once. Then I read it again. Then I read it for a third time because I do tend to get easily confused.

On this occasion, however, I was anything but. The message may have been short, but it couldn't have been any sweeter if I'd soaked it in chocolate and then sprinkled it with sugar.

> *Come to the SICK Bucket.*
> *Now.*
> *As in NOW!*
> *The Big Cheese.*
> *P.S. Where are you?*

To most ordinary people the message meant absolutely nothing, but then I'm not most ordinary people. Some days I'm not even a person. I'm more than that – don't ask me what; I'm making a lot of this up as I go along.

Now, feel free to take notes (and then guard them with your life) because what I'm about to tell you is strictly confidential.

SICK stands for Special Investigations into the Criminal Kind.

The SICK Bucket is its underground headquarters.

The Big Cheese is the top banana at SICK. Numero uno. The Chief.

Lesson complete. You may continue reading – or do something else entirely. Maybe a spot of wet paint watching. It's your choice. I'm not really fussed either way.

'Word of warning,' said the postman, although I half-expected his warning would consist of more than one word. 'That message will set alight in exactly five seconds ... *four ... three ... two ...*'

I slipped the paper onto my tongue and swallowed before he could finish his countdown. A moment later I felt a burning sensation rising in my chest. I burped and a plume of smoke blew out of both nostrils. By the time the smoke had cleared, the postman had vanished into thin air. Or maybe he had just walked off. Either way he had gone, leaving me free to jump to my feet and dance a happy little jig.

This was the news I had been waiting for all my life. Well, for the past few weeks at least. Against my mother's wishes, my father had secured me a position at SICK. I was following in his footsteps, although I had no intention of pouring cups of tea for the rest of my life. No, I was destined for more than that. Much, much more.

I, Hugo Dare, was going to be a spy.

5.'THE BIG CHEESE
IS READY FOR YOU.'

The day had dawned by the time I arrived at my destination.

As usual, the weather in Crooked Elbow was a combination of the three *d's* – dull, damp and depressingly dismal. The exact opposite to my mood, in fact. At that very moment, I was hopping about like a gorilla in a banana box (albeit a gorilla in his dressing gown and pyjamas because he hadn't had time to change).

And it was all because I had been summoned by the Big Cheese with (fingers crossed) the promise of good news.

Good news that (fingers crossed again) involved me becoming one of his spies.

The destination I arrived at – Takeaway Way – wasn't the grottiest part of Crooked Elbow – that was undoubtedly Elbow's Edge – but it was still an area that most people with even a smidgen of common sense would steer clear of. I, naturally, ignored any such logic and wandered there of my own free will.

Travel back in time and every last one of the tall, three-storey buildings that surrounded me had been home to some kind of eatery; whether it be a restaurant, a cafe, or, you've guessed it, a takeaway.

These days, however, things were a little different.

Only half the buildings were still occupied, whilst the other half had been boarded-up ready for demolition. The final half (*three halves?* I might have to check that) had gone one step further and were now missing both their doors and windows and even the occasional roof. In total, there were two hundred and twelve of these dilapidated dwellings, but I was only concerned with number sixty-six.

The Impossible Pizza.

If you didn't know better you would assume it had fallen on hard times and been forced to shut down. For a business to shut down, though, it has to be open to begin with. And The Impossible Pizza had never been open. Not even for a day.

Remembering everything my father had shown me, I grabbed the doorknob and turned it three times to my left and then twice to my right. There was a loud *click* and the door opened.

So far, so good.

I stuck my head in first and looked around. There was a counter directly in front of me with a price list above it decorated with images of various pizzas. Again, it was all for show. As were the ovens. I could smell they had been used recently, but there was no sign of the head chef and SICK's first line of defence, Impossible Rita. Rita had jet-black hair that had been cropped short, wild eyes and an even wilder temper. My father had warned me about her on many occasions. And, more importantly, what she would do to anybody who dared to enter The Impossible Pizza without her permission.

With that in mind, I crept forward on the toes of my slippers, careful not to make a sound. Somehow, I made it all the way to the counter without alerting Rita to my arrival. Now all I had to do was reach over and find the secret button and I had done it.

If only it was that easy.

'*D'yer wanna' pizza me?*'

In one swift motion, Rita leapt up onto the counter and then threw herself at me. Before I knew it, I was laid flat-out on my back, unable to move, powerless to fight back.

'D'yer wanna' pizza me?' Rita repeated, her hands squeezed tight around my neck.

My lips were flapping, but nothing came out. Panic-stricken, I pointed at my throat.

'Oh.' Rita loosened her grip. 'Too much?'

'Just … a … bit,' I panted. 'And, no, I do not want a piece of you, but I do want a pizza. That's as long as you make it a … *SICK special!*'

That was the code word. As soon as I said it, Rita let go and I could finally breathe.

'I've got a meeting with the Big Cheese,' I said, struggling to sit up. 'My name is Hugo Dare, but you're probably more familiar with my father, Dirk Dare.'

'The tea boy?' asked Rita.

'That's the chap,' I said. 'Although I prefer to call him the greatest spy who never was.'

'You might ... but I don't!' Rita held out her hand and pulled me up off the floor. 'I can't promise I won't jump on you the next time we meet,' she warned me.

'Oh, I'm hoping there'll be lots of *next times*,' I said excitedly. 'Especially once I become a spy.'

With the thought of attacking me on a regular basis ringing in her ears, Rita vaulted back over the counter and pressed the secret button that was hidden underneath. The building gently shook as a small, squared-shaped hole appeared in the wall to my right. It was the entrance to the rubbish chute.

And the only way I knew to get into the SICK Bucket.

I gave Rita a little wave and then climbed into the chute feet first, careful to hold on to the sides in case I fell.

That all changed, however, when I sneezed and let go by accident.

All of a sudden, I was hurtling downwards at a speed so terrifying it made my eyebrows stand on end. Thankfully, nothing lasts forever and the rubbish chute did nothing to dispel that theory.

My landing, when it came, was soft and squishy and, perhaps most surprising of all, human. Not only was Roland '*Rumble*' Robinson a silent giant of a security guard *and* one-time Crooked Elbow wrestling champion, but he also acted as a trampoline-cum-safety net for new arrivals. Sure enough, he set to work as soon as he had put me back on my feet. Spreading my arms and legs, he gave me one of his special *cuddles*. Or maybe it was an all-over body search. Either way, it gave me ample opportunity to cast an eye over my new surroundings.

I *could* tell you that the inside of SICK's secret headquarters were strictly state of the art, eye-poppingly shiny and built to the highest possible spec imaginable.

Similarly, I could tell you that I spend most evenings pretending to be a squirrel.

Neither would be true.

Quite simply, the SICK Bucket consisted of a series of narrow underground tunnels hidden beneath several buildings, one of which just happened to be The Impossible Pizza. The ceiling was held up by thick concrete pillars and there were a smattering of rooms scattered around the edges. The lighting was low and the slightest noise seemed to echo for well over a minute. It was a cold, soulless place, but then I had spent much of my young life stalking the corridors of Crooked Comp' so that was nothing new to me.

Cuddling complete, my first port of call was the Big Cheese's glamorous secretary, Miss Felicity Finefellow. We had only met a few times, but I already knew that Finefellow and I had a *thing*. What kind of *thing* I'm not entirely sure, but I could feel it in the air, hovering over us like a giant water balloon, ready to burst at any moment.

'Oh, it's you!' Dressed in a smart navy jacket and matching skirt, Finefellow's legs were crossed and she was filing her nails (toe not finger). 'I was hoping it might be someone not quite so abnormal,' she muttered.

'I bet you say that to all the boys,' I said, fluttering my eyelashes in her direction.

'No, just you,' said Finefellow bluntly. She lowered her head and a mass of cascading curls rolled over her face. For a moment I forgot how to breathe. That was the effect she had on me.

When the breath eventually came, it sounded as if I was choking.

'Please tell me that you're *not* alright,' said Finefellow, glancing up at me. I didn't reply, but instead gave her my best smile. All teeth *and* gums. My eyes, however, strayed towards her chin. Yes, you did read that correctly. *Her chin.*

Secrets of a Spy Number 22 – never trust a man – or woman – with a beard.

Thankfully, Finefellow didn't have any facial hair to speak of, but she did have smoky eyes, razor-sharp cheekbones and a voice like chocolate melting on a radiator. No, not a sticky mess – I mean warm and gooey. All of this was wrapped up in a wonderful haze of perfume. *Strong* perfume. As if she'd splashed it all over like vinegar on chips.

'Now, I know I'm not exactly boyfriend material—' I began.

'There's no *not exactly* about it!' interrupted Finefellow. 'You're only eleven—'

'Thirteen,' I said, correcting her.

Finefellow shook her head. 'You're still at school—'

'Not today, I'm not,' I said smugly.

'And you've got an incredibly unpleasant face,' she added. 'It's like a wasp that's been squashed against a car window. All scrunched up. Quite hideous really.'

Ever the gentleman, I laughed at Finefellow's poor attempt at humour, before she followed it up with some genuine concern.

'You're not normally so ugly, are you?' she said. 'What happened? Did somebody hit you in the face with a door?'

'How did you know?' I said, stunned. 'Were you there?'

'I wish,' grinned Finefellow.

'So do I.' I placed my hand on her desk, but my arm gave way (pesky weak elbows) and I fell nose first onto a hole punch. 'If you were there you could've rubbed it better,' I groaned.

'I don't touch worms,' said Finefellow, backing away from me. At the same time she pointed over her shoulder at a door marked *The Pantry*. 'The Big Cheese is ready for you,' she said. 'You can go in anytime you want … although, for obvious reasons, I'd prefer it if you went in sooner rather than later!'

With that, Finefellow grabbed one of her high heels and used it to poke me in the rib cage. I took this as my cue to leave and headed towards the only door behind her. I knocked once but didn't wait for a reply.

Instead, I walked straight into the lion's den.

Or, in this case, the Big Cheese's Pantry.

6. 'SPY!'

Let's get two things straight.

The Big Cheese's Pantry isn't really a pantry in the same way that the Big Cheese isn't really an enormous chunk of cheddar. It's an office. And he's just a man. I hope that's cleared things up for those of you who can't read between the lines.

I'd entered the Pantry once before, but I'd never actually met the Big Cheese. In hindsight, the Big Cheese may have been hiding. In double hindsight, hiding places are seriously limited in the Pantry. That was due largely to its size. Or lack of it. It's small, you see. Smaller than small. *Little more than a store cupboard* small. Although I'm fairly certain that there's nothing stored in it. Okay, so it's just a cupboard then.

Phew. Got there in the end, didn't we?

Stood in the doorway, I considered my options in four easy steps.

Step one and I'd bump into a stiff-looking piece of red moulded plastic. The visitor's chair.

Step two and I'd bang my knees on an antique wooden

writing table that was piled high with pizza boxes.

Step three and I'd have by-passed both the table and its companion, a leather armchair, only to find myself nose-to-brick with the opposite wall.

Step four and … oh, that's not possible. Not without a pneumatic drill at least.

So, where was the Big Cheese?

I sniffed the air, my nostrils flaring at the unmistakable stench of old fish and sea water. That had to belong to him, although for obvious reasons I had expected something a little *cheesier*. Don't get me wrong; it wasn't an overly unpleasant pong. Just nothing worth bottling up and selling as a fragrance.

'Note to self,' I muttered out loud. 'There's no money in the stink of Big Cheese.'

'My stink is not – and will never be – for sale!'

The pizza boxes piled up on the table flew to one side as an enormous face appeared in their place.

Walrus.

That was the first thought that crossed my mind. Not that I'd ever seen one before. Not in Crooked Elbow, anyway.

I looked again.

Okay, so maybe it was just a man who looked like a walrus. He did, after all, have a square, balding head, round eyes, huge teeth, and, most prominent of all, a thick, droopy moustache that hung down below his chin.

Secrets of a Spy Number 23 – moustaches are fine (even on a woman). It's just beards you need to be wary of.

The walrus man was dressed in a tweed jacket with matching waistcoat and silk cravat. It was a seriously strong *look*. A powerful look. A look that demanded respect. I knew without being told that I was in the company of Cheese.

And it was Big.

'Good morning, sir,' I mumbled. Nerves must have got the better of me because I forgot how to bow and instead gave a little curtsy. 'This is a great—'

'*Pleasure!*' boomed the Big Cheese. His voice was deep, almost as if he had a tuba lodged at the back of his throat. 'And so it should be, you pyjama wearing prune. One question, though. Who the devil are you, what the devil do you want, and why the devil are you trying to steal my stink?'

His one question had multiplied at such an alarming rate that I chose to ignore it completely. 'You summoned me, sir,' I replied, 'although not from the bowels of Hell like you seem to imagine.'

'Summoned you?' The Big Cheese grabbed at one of the pizza boxes and took out a slice. Beetroot and watermelon by the smell of things. Unusual yet undeniably delicious. 'Name?' barked the Big Cheese, as he took an enormous bite.

'Yes, sir,' I nodded, 'but then hasn't everybody?'

'No, you dribbling duck egg!' the Big Cheese bellowed. '*What* is your name? Who are you?'

'Not who, sir … *Hugo*,' I explained. 'Hugo Dare. My father is—'

'Dirk Dare!' There was a moment of confusion on the Big Cheese's face before he tossed the rest of the pizza over his shoulder in delight. 'Ah, so you're young Dare,' he cried.

'They told me you were different – just not *this* different. Still, any son of old Dare is fine by me. Your father and I go back a long way. At least two-and-a-half miles.'

'Dirk Dare is the greatest spy who never was,' I said proudly.

'Dirk Dare is the greatest tea boy who *is!*' argued the Big Cheese. 'Twenty-one years he's worked under me here in the SICK Bucket and his teapot has never let him down. Now, you don't look like much, young Dare, but if you're half the man your father is—'

'Then I'll be extremely small,' I said.

'Exactly,' agreed the Big Cheese. 'Your father's not the tallest of chaps, is he? Or the thinnest. As for you, don't just stand there looking gormless. Take a seat.'

'Take it where, sir?' I wondered.

'Take it for your bottom,' instructed the Big Cheese. 'Park your rear. Sit.'

I did as he asked and went to plonk myself down on the chunk of plastic beside me. Unfortunately, my aim was a little off and I missed it completely.

'On your feet, young Dare!' hollered the Big Cheese. 'If you're going to work for me then you can't spend your days rolling about on the carpet.'

I leapt up in a flash. '*Work for you, sir?*' I said excitedly. 'You mean … you mean …?'

The Big Cheese nodded. 'Indeed, I do.'

'I'm going to be a … a …' I stammered.

The Big Cheese nodded again. 'Yes, you're going to be a—'

'*Spy!*' I blurted out.

'Toilet boy,' said the Big Cheese.

My legs gave way and I sank back down to the carpet. 'Toilet boy?'

'There's no need to look so disappointed,' the Big Cheese insisted. 'Toilet boy is a highly prestigious position within SICK. You might not believe this, but your duties will be both challenging and rewarding. If the toilet is dirty, you clean it. If the toilet is blocked, you unblock it. If somebody tries to steal the toilet, you steal it back. Many of our finest spies have started out on their hands and knees, armed only with a bottle of bleach and a pair of rubber gloves.'

'*Really?*' I said, shocked. 'Were you a toilet boy, sir?'

'*Me?*' The Big Cheese threw back his head and roared with laughter. 'Don't talk such nonsense! I'm far too important for that.' He was still laughing when Miss Finefellow entered the Pantry. 'Did you hear that, Felicity? Young Dare wondered if I'd ever been a toilet boy. How ridiculous!'

'Indeed, sir,' nodded Finefellow. 'Although nowhere near as ridiculous as what I'm about to tell you now. Your agents are falling like bowling pins. We've lost four already this morning.'

'Lost four agents?' The Big Cheese bounced his forehead off the table in disbelief. 'That's a bit careless. Who was looking after them?'

'You were,' sighed Finefellow. She drew a breath before reeling off the list. 'Agents Fifteen and Sixteen have run off to open a florists together; Agent Twenty-Six has been trampled on by a herd of stampeding buffalo and Agent

Nine got her scarf caught in a tumble-dryer ... *whilst she was still wearing it!* None of them will be returning to work ... *ever!* Finefellow pouted her lips in despair. 'This can't go on, sir,' she said. 'We need more agents. We can advertise ... definitely online ... maybe in the newspaper ... or—'

'*Not!*' cried the Big Cheese. 'We haven't got time to wait for applicants and interviews and teaching and training. We're desperate, Felicity. We've got a hole that needs filling. If only I could find someone with superb *hole-filling* abilities.'

I sat up, elated. 'Look no further, sir.'

'You, young Dare!' blasted the Big Cheese. 'You're about as much use as an empty crisp packet in a hurricane!'

I sat back down, deflated.

'At least, that was what I thought when I first met you.' The Big Cheese stopped and pulled on his moustache. 'Maybe I was wrong,' he admitted. 'Maybe there is more to you than meets the eye.'

'There's not, sir,' said Finefellow. 'There's actually *less* to Dare than meets the eye.'

'Maybe you could help out until the dust has settled,' continued the Big Cheese, ignoring his secretary. 'How does that grab you, young Dare? Would you like to be one of my agents?'

I didn't reply. Not at first. My ears had lied to me so many times before that they couldn't be trusted. 'One of your agents, sir?' I asked.

'That's right,' nodded the Big Cheese, snatching at a fresh slice of pizza. 'Say yes and, from this day forth, you'll be the spy who came in from the toilet.'

7.'TO DO IS TO DARE AND TO DARE IS TO DO.'

Miss Finefellow began to stamp her feet.

Don't panic; they weren't on fire. It was just a desperate bid to grab the Big Cheese's attention.

'Do you think that's wise, sir?' she cried. 'Do you really want to make this ... *creature* one of your agents?'

'Probably not,' shrugged the Big Cheese. His fingers fumbled inside the pizza box for his third slice in less than a minute. 'Young Dare isn't my first choice. He's not even my second choice. But he is here. And that makes him a better choice than somebody who isn't. You can't argue with that, Felicity.'

'Can't I, sir?' With that, Finefellow turned sharply and left the Pantry, stopping only to slam the door behind her.

'Yes,' I said, once the walls had stopped shaking. 'In answer to your question, sir, I would like to be a spy. More than anything.'

'In that case, welcome to SICK, Agent Minus Thirty-Five,' boomed the Big Cheese.

'Agent Minus Thirty-Five?' It took all my powers of concentration, but I finally managed to clamber up off the carpet and master the art of sitting in a chair. 'Great joke, sir,' I said. 'A proper rip-snorter. So, what number agent am I really? *Three? Five? Eight?* I'm in the top ten, right? *Not right?* Okay … how about … *thirteen? Sixteen-and-a-half?* Anything higher than that and I can't promise I'll leave quietly—'

'You are Agent Minus Thirty-Five and you shall stay Agent Minus Thirty-Five until further notice,' declared the Big Cheese. 'You should feel honoured. I've just promoted you about eight levels in SICK in the space of two minutes. Carry on like that and you'll have my job by lunchtime.' The Big Cheese stopped chewing and closed the pizza box. I figured he had something important to say. 'These are dark times, young Dare,' he began. 'Dark, dark times.'

'Would you like me to turn the light on, sir?' I suggested.

'If only it was that simple,' the Big Cheese sighed.

'I think you'll find it is,' I said. 'One click of a switch and—'

'This has got nothing to do with light bulbs!' barked the Big Cheese. 'It's much more complicated than that. I've got a mission that requires an agent with no special qualities whatsoever. I need an unknown. A non-entity. The sort of person you would choose to ignore even if they were stood on your shoelaces.'

'*Wow!* That's some barrel you're scraping, sir,' I said. 'Where do you think you'll find such a loser?'

'In the toilet, of course!' the Big Cheese laughed.

And that was when I realised he was talking about me.

'Don't look like that,' insisted the Big Cheese. 'You're perfect for my mission. *Perfectly anonymous*. You don't walk like a spy, you don't talk like a spy and you certainly don't look like a spy. You'll be able to drift through Crooked Elbow without a second glance. You're a complete nobody ... *and that's the best thing about you!*'

'Thank you, sir ... *I think*,' I said. 'So, what is it that you want this *complete nobody* to do?'

'One of my agents is about to explode,' revealed the Big Cheese. 'Not literally, of course. But he is being over-worked and we can't afford to lose him like the others. I'm referring to Agent One.'

'*Agent One?*' I said, screwing up my face. 'That's a bit better than Agent Minus Thirty-Five.'

'And that's because Agent One is a bit better than you,' replied the Big Cheese. 'In fact, he's the finest agent we have. Your mission, young Dare, is to get out there and assist him in any way you can. Keep your head down, your mouth shut and your eyes and ears open. Just do what Agent One tells you and try not to think for yourself. And, most important of all, don't get in the way.'

'As if I would,' I said. 'You can rely on me, sir. I'll do my best to help the best.'

'*Don't!*' cried the Big Cheese. 'I need you to do someone else's best. Someone whose best is a lot better than yours. Now, take a look at this ...' The Chief of SICK removed a photograph from his waistcoat and pushed it across the table. 'I want you to familiarise yourself with Agent One.'

Aged somewhere between middle and old (*mould?*), the

man in the photograph was handsome in a movie star kind of way with a fantastic head of fluffy grey hair, piercing blue eyes and sharp, chiselled features. The most striking thing about him, however, were his teeth. Perfectly proportioned as if they'd been carved by hand, they were so dazzlingly white that, come nightfall, they could easily have illuminated the whole of Crooked Elbow with even the faintest of smiles.

'His codename is Silver Fox,' revealed the Big Cheese. 'Even as we speak he's deep undercover trying to infiltrate a dangerous gang of bank robbers. As far as I'm aware both sides are communicating, but are still yet to meet. Nevertheless, Fox is sure that the thieves will strike soon. The most likely target is the Bottle Bank. I myself have an account there.'

'I tend to keep my pennies in a pair of my father's socks,' I said. 'They were hanging on the washing line the last time I looked. Perfectly safe.'

'I'm sure they are,' frowned the Big Cheese. 'Back to Fox, and in the past few days his trail has gone worryingly cold. I can't seem to make contact with him and, if I'm being honest, I'm not entirely sure where he is or what's going on. His last known address was a room that you pay for ... surrounded by lots of other rooms ... on many floors ... in a very tall building.'

'Like ... *a hotel?*' I guessed.

'Exactly like a hotel,' nodded the Big Cheese. 'It's called the Hard Times Hotel to be precise. It's a rotten establishment frequented by rogues and wrong 'uns of the lowest order. Danger lurks behind every dustbin, so don't draw attention to yourself and try to remain undercover at all times.'

Undercover. The word alone was enough to make my belly button dance with delight. 'This is all well and good, sir,' I said, 'but surely I'll need something to help me with my mission. I'm thinking gadgets—'

'And I'm thinking not!' hollered the Big Cheese. 'You're a complete nobody, young Dare. And complete nobodys do not have gadgets.'

'How about a disguise then?' I said. 'Some fake teeth would be good. Maybe I could borrow yours—'

'And maybe you can't!' snapped the Big Cheese. 'No, you need to blend in, not stand out with an enormous set of gnashers poking out of your mouth. With that in mind, I'd advise you to ditch that dressing gown as well. And your name. *Young Dare.* That'll never do. Like all my other agents, you'll need a codename. I've thought long and hard about this for less than a second and decided upon Pink Weasel.'

'*Pink Weasel?*' I repeated it several times, rolling it around my tongue until I almost swallowed it by accident. 'I love it, sir,' I said eventually.

'Splendid,' nodded the Big Cheese, 'because from now on that'll be how you introduce yourself to everyone you meet. Now, get out of my Pantry and find Silver Fox before I see sense and send you back to the toilet.'

'Consider me gone, sir.' Jumping up, I opened the door and took the one step it required for me to be true to my word.

'One last thing,' the Big Cheese called out. 'This is a big

chapter in your life, young Dare. To do is to dare and to dare is to do. Do I make myself clear?'

'Not in the slightest, sir,' I said honestly, 'but I'll be sure to bear it in mind.'

Bending my knees, I gave the Big Cheese another curtsy before I finally exited the Pantry. His words, however, were still bouncing around my brain as I crawled back up the rubbish chute. It may have been a big chapter in my life, but this certainly isn't a big chapter in the book. A few pages at best.

It was time to move on. Destination: the Hard Times Hotel.

I had a Silver Fox to sniff out.

8.'AFTER YOU, WRINKLES.'

I left the SICK Bucket via The Impossible Pizza, avoiding Impossible Rita in the process.

Before I set off for the Hard Times Hotel, however, I had a slight detour to make. The Big Cheese's instructions had been clear. *Ditch the dressing gown.* So that was what I did as soon as I arrived back home.

I ditched it and replaced it with my father's dressing gown instead.

Longer in length and brown in colour, it was far less extravagant than my own luminous yellow effort. Not only that, but it was also perfect for those moments when I needed to hide behind a huge pile of mud. And, as every good spy knows, moments like that are never too far away.

There was a third reason why I chose my father's dressing gown, but for now I'll keep it to myself. Don't fret; all will be revealed in due course. About fifty thousand words at last count. That's if we both make it that far.

Fully dressed and raring to go, there was still one last thing I had to grab before I left the house.

My mother's umbrella.

I found it on the coat stand by the door. It was hardly a disguise, but it was as close to one as I was going to get. Now all I needed was for the rain to arrive.

And, thankfully, it did.

Secrets of a Spy Number 11 – in a world where people cannot be trusted, the rain is your greatest ally.

Let me explain. By the time I had made my way to the Hard Times Hotel, the clouds that hung constantly over Crooked Elbow had begun to unleash a torrent of droplets so heavy that all who dared to linger beneath them for even a millisecond were immediately soaked to the skin. Umbrella or not, nobody with even an ounce of noggin juice was crazy enough to be taking a stroll out in this kind of weather.

Nobody except me.

As a spy, this was to my advantage. A crowded street and you have no idea who may be creeping up on you, ready to attack. If the street is empty then the only person you have to worry about is yourself. And, believe me, *I* was already enough for me to worry about.

I came to a halt at a bus stop directly opposite the hotel and took shelter under the sign. My plan was simple. If Silver Fox was inside the building then at some point he would have to come out. I didn't mind waiting. Not in the slightest. The art of spying is all about patience, after all. If I wanted I could stand there for hours ... days ... weeks ... months ...

Seventy-three seconds later and boredom had kicked in. Twenty-one seconds after that and I had actually nodded off, only to be woken by the loud *grumble* of a passing bus. Still half-asleep, I rubbed my eyes and looked over at the hotel.

There was a man stood in the entrance.

At first glance, he seemed to vaguely resemble Silver Fox if Silver Fox wasn't really Silver Fox. In other words, gone were the movie star looks, only to be replaced by an unkempt mop of hair, a weather-beaten face and a chin that was covered in stubble. Add to that a faded leather jacket and dirty jeans and, at best, the man could only be described as Agent One on a really bad day.

Hidden beneath my mother's umbrella, I watched as the *maybe* Silver Fox peered up at the dreary rainclouds and began to yawn. As he did so, there was a dazzling glow. Ah, yes, that confirmed my suspicions. His outward appearance may have let him down, but Silver Fox's teeth remained as white as ever. In fact, if he kept his mouth open any longer, people would be fooled into thinking that the sun had come out. And the sun never came out in Crooked Elbow. That was a fact. First page in the Crooked Elbow rule book (the second page consists largely of ways to eat spaghetti).

Yawn over, Silver Fox turned to his right and headed towards an old-fashioned telephone box not far from the hotel entrance. He ducked inside and the phone began to ring. Fox picked it up, listened for a moment and then put it back on its hook. He left the box immediately and walked back to the hotel. Then he was gone. The whole thing, from start to finish, had lasted less than a minute.

Mindful of any passing milk floats, I dashed across the road. If I didn't follow him inside the hotel I risked losing him altogether. And that was something I couldn't let happen. Not on my first day.

THE GREATEST SPY WHO NEVER WAS

My route, however, was blocked as soon as I reached the other side.

Shuffling along at a pace even a snail would've been ashamed of, was an elderly lady with an enormous knitting bag. Dressed in a long black cloak, the hood of which was pulled tight over a particularly gruesome face that could easily have passed for a mask at Halloween, her shoulders were hunched and her steps were few as she struggled towards the hotel entrance.

I sped up and swerved to my left, managing, somehow, to get there before her.

'After you, Wrinkles,' I said, stepping to one side as I opened the door.

I wasn't expecting much in return. A *thank you* perhaps. Or even a toothless grin.

What I *didn't* expect, however, was for Wrinkles to strike me firmly over the head with her knitting bag.

I didn't see it coming, but I certainly felt it. Whatever was in that bag, it was far heavier than a ball of wool (unless the wool was still attached to the sheep, of course).

'My pleasure,' I whimpered. The urge became too great and I stuck my head inside my father's dressing gown so I could scream out loud. When I finally removed it, Wrinkles had vanished. Hopefully for good. Never to be seen again.

If only that was true …

9.'YOU CAN CALL ME PINKY.'

Steadying myself with the aid of my mother's umbrella, I put all thoughts of Crooked Elbow's most violent pensioner to the back of my mind as I entered the Hard Times Hotel.

If first impressions counted for anything then I should really have turned around and walked straight back out again. The wallpaper in the lobby was peeling and the carpet was practically non-existent. There were patches of mould in every corner (not to mention several corners that didn't even exist) and numerous buckets scattered randomly about the floor. The buckets were there to catch the drips and drops that fell from the ceiling. Drips and drops of what exactly I wasn't entirely sure, but it was highly unlikely to be rainwater.

'*Welcome to the Hard Times Hotel. My name is Coco. How can I be of assistance?*'

I looked around for any sign of a reception desk, but all I could see was a telephone, on what remained of the carpet, with an over-grown carrot sat cross-legged beside it. On closer inspection, carrots don't usually have legs (or any other bodily features come to that) so I guessed it was a human.

Older than me but younger than Wrinkles (that narrows it down a bit), the human in question had green hair that seemed to explode from the top of her head and a bright orange face that was caked in a layer of make-up so thick that she must've applied it using the cricket bat technique.

Close your eyes, swing your arms and hope for the best.

Curiously, it's the same technique I use when visiting the lavatory.

'*Welcome to the Hard Times Hotel. My name is Coco. How can I be of assistance?*'

Her voice reminded me of a dentist's drill. No, make that *two* dentists' drills. On full power. As I walked towards her, a slightly putrid stench wafted up from where she sat. It was the smell of tanning lotion. If nothing else it explained why Coco was more the colour of a satsuma than an actual satsuma.

'Welcome to the Hard Times Hotel. My name is Coco. How can I– … oh, what do you want, boy? And don't say a room 'cos we ain't got none available.'

'No, it's not a room I'm after,' I replied. 'It's a man.'

'Aren't we all,' sighed Coco. 'Not easy round here, mind. Most of the men in Crooked Elbow are rotten from top to bottom.'

'The man I'm looking for isn't,' I said. 'He's positively … *rotten-less*. His name is …' Ah, problem. I had no idea what name Agent One had checked in under. '*Mr Fox*,' I guessed.

The words had barely left my lips when Coco jumped up and grabbed me by my father's dressing gown. For one awful moment I thought she was going to kiss me. Thankfully, that moment passed and all she did was whisper in my ear. 'You want to watch yourself.'

'I didn't think that was possible,' I said. 'Not without a mirror.'

'Mr Fox ain't just a pretty face,' continued Coco. 'He's ... *shifty*. Always coming and going ... as if he's up to something ... something devious. I don't trust him as far as I can throw him.'

'I'll be sure to pass on your kind regards,' I said, eager to hurry things along a bit. 'Although to do that I'll first have to know which room he's staying in.'

'You're making a big mistake,' said Coco, as she sat back down on the carpet.

'I've made bigger,' I shrugged. 'Besides, it's hardly the end of the world.'

'Could be,' muttered Coco. 'The end of *your* world. Still, I'm not one to interfere. I'm just a simple receptionist.'

'A *very* simple receptionist,' I said, looking around the lobby. 'You've not even got a desk.'

'It was stolen,' said Coco sadly. 'Along with my computer. And my stool. Now it's just me and my telephone.' Coco pointed at the ceiling. 'You'll find Mr Fox on the fourth floor. Room *404* to be precise. Don't say I didn't warn you, though.'

Armed with the information I required, I was all set to bid Coco farewell when I was struck by a sudden mind movement. 'What about Wrinkles?'

'*Wrinkles?* Coco put her hands up to her face in horror. 'I've never had a wrinkle in my life!'

'Not your wrinkles,' I said, much to Coco's relief. 'I'm

talking about that wrinkly old walnut who wandered in here a few seconds before me.'

'No one came in before you,' insisted Coco. 'Only Mr Fox, but he's always in and out—' She was stopped mid-sentence by the sound of her ringing telephone. 'I have to get that ... *erm* ... what's your name again?'

'Weasel,' I replied. 'Pink Weasel. But you can call me *Pinky*.'

With that, I left Coco to her duties and made my way across the hotel lobby. It seemed strange that she had failed to notice Wrinkles, but I didn't dwell on it for long. If anything, I was far more interested in the fact that I had added an extra *Y* to my codename. From now on, I was Pinky. And I liked it.

I could've stopped when I reached the lift, but chose, instead, to carry on towards the staircase.

Secrets of a Spy Number 19 – always use the longest route available to get to your destination.

Think about it. The longer the journey, the more time you have to plan for whatever lay in wait. If I'm being honest, it did once back-fire when I tested it at home. Still, I can't be the only one who's wet themselves midway through a five-mile trip to the bathroom.

Can I?

Four flights of stairs later I was on my knees; panting for the breath that had long since deserted me. I stayed that way whilst I took in my surroundings. The corridor on the fourth floor was about as well presented as the lobby (not very), but with even more buckets for the drips and a far greater array of exposed electrical wires hanging down from the ceiling.

The way things were going, it was a race to see whether the hotel would flood or burn down first. My money (if I had any) was on a combination of the two. Preferably only once I'd departed, though.

Back on my feet, I set off in search of Room *404*. The door nearest to me had *401* carved into the wood so I knew I was close. I walked forward and heard screaming coming from inside *402*. Then something that could easily have passed for a gunshot – or just a particularly loud sneeze – from *403*.

Two more steps and I was there.

Room *404*.

The door was open. Not just slightly ajar, but pushed firmly to one side and then left there as if it was no longer required. I had never met Silver Fox, but I figured that no respectable spy would leave a door in such a manner. Not even an *unrespectable* one.

I crouched down and pretended to tie my shoelace. It's not easy when you're wearing slippers, but I carried on regardless. Whilst I was down there I turned my head for a sneaky peek into *404*.

Wow!

The room was in such a state that it was impossible to know where to look first. And when I say *such a state*, I don't just mean a little bit messy. No, from floor to ceiling, it had been completely ransacked. The bed had been flipped over, the corners of the carpet had been peeled back and the bedside table had been sliced and diced into tiny chunks of firewood.

I remained in my *shoelaces* position and shuffled sideways. The closer I got to *404*, the worse it seemed to get. The wardrobe was balancing on its side, whilst the television had been smashed in half. I kept moving, over the threshold, until I was inside the room. As I did so, the feeling grew that I was about to stumble upon something ugly at any moment.

Something *very* ugly.

And, sure enough, I did.

10. 'DON'T LET HER IN!'

The man I knew to be Silver Fox was hidden behind the upturned bed.

He was alone. *Almost.* He had a chair for company, which he had decided to sit on, although probably not through choice given that his eyes were blindfolded and his hands were tied behind his back.

Oh, and he was also completely naked except for a pair of tiny, white underpants.

'Don't mind me,' I said, shielding my eyes. 'Maybe I should just leave you to it ...'

Silver Fox didn't reply, although that was hardly surprising seeing as there was a thick black sock stuffed inside his mouth. Not only that, but his chin was resting on his chest and he didn't appear to be breathing. All things considered, it was hardly a good look for someone who, less than a few minutes ago, had been wandering around outside the hotel.

'Are you dead?' I whispered. It wasn't the best question to ask. Especially if the answer just happened to be *yes*.

Thankfully, it wasn't. But then it wasn't a *no* either. It

was more a vow of silence.

Try again, Hugo.

Lifting Fox's head up by his chin, I carefully removed the sock from his mouth before using my favourite finger (index on my right hand) to flick him firmly on the nose.

His nostrils twitched not once, but four times.

'*Who's there?*' he called out.

'Not who – *Hugo*,' I said. 'Don't thank me now, but I'm your knight in shining armour. Without the armour. And the rest of me's not that shiny either.'

'There's somebody here!' cried Fox. 'In the room!'

'Of course there is,' I laughed. '*Me.*'

'Not you!' Fox began to shake his head, making it impossible for me to remove his blindfold. 'Somebody else!'

I sensed movement behind me. Pirouetting on the spot like an over-eager ballerina, I saw that Silver Fox was telling the truth. There was a third person in the room. And they were even uglier than Agent One in his underpants.

It was Wrinkles. My ancient attacker from the hotel entrance. Her hood was up and her head was down. And she was still dragging that same enormous knitting bag.

Armed and dangerous. Just how I *didn't* like her.

'Come to apologise, have we?' I said, breaking the silence. 'A simple sorry should do the trick.'

Wrinkles didn't reply. Instead, she shuffled towards me, both hands gripped tightly around her weapon of choice.

'Don't let her in!' begged Fox.

'It's too late for that,' I said, turning to face him. 'She's *in* already.'

'Then get her out!' Fear seemed to suddenly take hold as Fox's hair turned another shade of grey. 'You don't understand,' he shouted. 'She's after my ... my—'

'Your *what?*' I asked. 'Your chair? Your blindfold? Not your ... *underpants?*'

'She's after my equipment!' yelled Fox.

'What equipment?' When I turned back, Wrinkles was closer than I expected. *Threateningly* close. As was her knitting bag. That was level with my head. Almost as if she was going to hit me with it.

Think again, Wrinkles.

Without missing a beat I did a double somersault followed by the splits. Or something like that. It happened so fast it's hard to remember. Maybe I just ducked. Or fell over. All that mattered was that the knitting bag missed me as it flew through the air.

The momentum left Wrinkles unsteady on her feet. As she staggered forwards, I saw my chance and dropped to one knee. I had a clear shot at her stomach. Pulling back my fist, I took aim and ...

Something held me back. Try as I might, I couldn't punch a grumpy old granny in the gut. What if all her bones exploded and she crumpled to the ground in a great gooey mess of cabbage and mothballs? Worse than that, what if some of it landed on my father's dressing gown? Or even in my mouth?

Unfortunately for yours truly, Wrinkles didn't feel the same way about striking me.

She swung again and the knitting bag caught me fair and

square on the temple. My eyes began to wobble before my knees gave way and I fell face-first onto the carpet. I was both dazed and confused in confusingly daze-like measures. I had lost all feeling. Feelings I had lost. One last question, though. From me to you. And then I'll be free to ... *go*.

Who ...
Turned ...
Out ...
The ...
Lights?

11.'WE ARE THE BOTTLE BROTHERS.'

I awoke to the strangest of sensations.

It was almost as if somebody was repeatedly kicking me in the face. Over and over and over again. Not so hard as to cause pain, but enough to bring me back to reality.

Reality being the Hard Times Hotel ... Silver Fox ... *Wrinkles!*

My eyes snapped open. The first thing I saw was a bare foot swinging back and forth in front of my nose. 'Do you have to do that?' I groaned.

At the sound of my voice, Silver Fox did the honourable thing and stopped using my head as a football. As far as I could tell, he was still strapped to the chair and I was laid out on the carpet in front of him. And, yes, he was still wearing nothing but a blindfold and a pair of underpants.

'How long have I been out for?' I asked.

'About two minutes,' Fox replied.

'*Two minutes?*' I said, struggling to sit up. 'It felt like longer. At least two-and-a-half. Has she gone yet?'

'You tell me,' muttered Fox. I took the hint and removed his blindfold. 'About time,' he said, squinting back at me. Once he could see properly, his eyes began to dart around the room. '*My equipment!*' he cried. '*It's been stolen!*'

'By Wrinkles?' I asked.

'If you mean that old woman, then yes,' nodded Fox. 'It was her who stripped off my clothes and tied me to this chair. Then she trashed my room. You disturbed her ... *but not for long!*' Fox looked me up and down. 'You seem familiar,' he said. 'Have we met before?'

'Obviously,' I said. 'A few minutes ago before I was knocked out.'

'No, somewhere else,' said Fox, thinking hard. 'Of course. I've seen you in the SICK Bucket. With the tea boy.'

'You mean Dirk Dare, the greatest spy who never was,' I said proudly.

'No, I'm pretty certain I mean the tea boy,' argued Fox.

'They're the same person,' I explained. 'I'm his son. Although, now I'm something else entirely. I'm like you. I'm a spy.'

'*A spy?*' Fox shook his head. 'I don't think so somehow.'

'It's true,' I said. 'I'm Agent Minus Thirty-Five.'

'There's no such number,' laughed Fox.

'I've even got a codename,' I said. 'It's Pink Weasel. But you can call me Pinky.'

'Is this some kind of weird dream?' wondered Fox. 'Or is it just a really bad nightmare? Pinch me so I can wake up.' I knew he wasn't asleep, but I pinched him regardless. 'Whoever you are, this is terrible timing on your part,' Fox continued. 'Two men are on their way here even as we speak. They'll want to see my equipment, but that's not going to happen. Not now it's been stolen. What I need you to do is free me from this chair and then get out. They're arriving at half-past-eleven so we haven't got long.'

I glanced up at the only thing in *404* that had managed to survive Wrinkles' destruction – the clock on the wall. 'We've got even less than that,' I said. 'It's half-past eleven now.'

'Then we're too late,' said a grim-faced Fox. 'They'll know there's something wrong as soon as—' He stopped suddenly at the sound of heavy footsteps outside in the corridor. 'They're here,' he whispered. '*Hide.*'

'I would if I could,' I said, peering around the room, 'but all the best hiding places seem to have been destroyed.'

Fox opened his mouth to speak again, but was beaten to it by the *crunch* of splintering wood as the door to *404* was pulled off its hinges and cast to one side.

Two identical men appeared in its place. Both were short and stocky in build and dressed head-to-toe in brown. Both had big, bald heads, pointy ears and tiny, piggy eyes. And both had faces that resembled a puddle of wet concrete on a cloudy day. In fact, the only real difference I could see between them was that the man on the left was wearing a pair of thick, horn-rimmed spectacles, whilst the man on the right was carrying a brown leather briefcase.

'Ah, room service,' I said, trying to play it cool. 'Do excuse the mess. We had a little accident involving a particularly angry pensioner and her not-so-friendly knitting bag.'

The two men grimaced at one another as they marched into the room.

'Ignore me,' I said, backing away. 'I always say daft things when I'm nervous. And I always get nervous when visitors choose to remove the door rather than knock on it.'

The man in the spectacles opened his mouth and revealed a set of brown teeth. So predictable.

'We are the Bottle Brothers,' he said gruffly. 'We own the Bottle Bank, Crooked Elbow's first and foremost financial institution for the disgustingly rich. My name is Boris. And this is Igor.'

'I can speak for myself, brother,' snarled Boris's briefcase-carrying twin. 'I am Igor, but my enemies call me Igor the Irritable.'

'You should try using a different washing powder,' I said. 'Less itchy.'

'I get irritable when I cannot hurt people,' Igor remarked.

'In that case, stop washing your clothes altogether,' I said hastily. 'Don't worry about the smell. I'm sure people will still find you perfectly pleasant when they get to know you—'

'No, they will not!' shot back Boris. 'My brother is not pleasant in the slightest. And neither am I. And we are not here to talk about washing powder. We are here to see Mr Fox—'

'*And Mr Fox only!*' added Igor menacingly.

I thought about how this must look to both bald-headed Bottles. One of us (me) was thirteen years old and dressed in yellow pyjamas and an over-sized dressing gown, whilst the other (Fox) was tied to a chair, wearing nothing but his underpants. To make matters worse, the room looked like a wrecking ball had hit it. Which it had, of course. A *wrinkly* wrecking ball.

'I am waiting,' said Boris.

'Me too,' agreed Igor.

'Me three,' I said. 'Just remind me, though. What is it that we're actually waiting for?'

'Which – of – you – is – Mr – Fox?' asked Boris. He spoke slowly as if I was extremely stupid. Which was strange because I didn't think he knew me that well.

By now the real Silver Fox's hair had virtually turned its back on grey altogether. He looked scared. Terrified even. Don't ask me why. He obviously had no idea who he was working with. Like a magician at a child's birthday party, I could pull a rabbit out of a top hat with nothing but a wave of my wand.

Although I don't actually own a top hat.

Or a wand.

And I think I may be allergic to rabbits.

So I'm nothing like a magician at all.

But I did have something up my sleeve.

Secrets of a Spy Number 25 – when answering a particularly awkward question, think of the most outrageous lie you can ... and then say it!

'I'm Mr Fox,' I announced, thrusting my hand out to be shaken. 'Let's get down to business.'

12. 'DO YOU WANT ME TO KILL HIM?'

I saw movement out of the corner of my eye.

It was Silver Fox. The *real* Silver Fox. He was about to speak and I couldn't let that happen.

Moving quickly, I grabbed the sock and shoved it back where I had first found it – in Fox's mouth – before he could say another word. Or, worse still, tell the truth.

'*You?*' said Boris Bottle, squeezing the one syllable out into something much longer. 'You are Mr Fox, the best vault-cracker in the whole of Crooked Elbow?'

I screwed up my face. '*Vault-cracker?* What's a vault-cracker?'

Boris made a noise like a bulldozer without its dozer. 'A vault-cracker opens vaults ... *obviously*,' he explained. 'In this case, our vault.'

'In our bank,' added Igor.

'Of course they do,' I said. 'I mean ... *I do*. Of course I do.'

'You informed us, Mr Fox, that you were the man... no,

the *boy* who could help us steal from the vault in the Bottle Bank,' continued Boris. 'Now, I hope that's true because if you've lied to us ...'

My head had started to spin before he had even finished his sentence. Not only was I now the best vault-cracker in the whole of Crooked Elbow, but I had also volunteered to help rob a bank! Silver Fox could've warned me about what I was letting myself in for (although, in fairness, maybe he couldn't. Not once I'd stuffed that sock back in his mouth.)

'Yes, it's true,' I said untruthfully. 'I'm all of that and more. And then a little bit more on top of that.'

'That is a lot of *more*,' muttered Boris. My knuckles cracked as he finally shook my hand. Before our fingers slipped apart, I took the chance to grab a full blast of his aroma. *Sawdust*. It made sense. A serious smell for a seriously serious person.

'It is nice, Mr Fox ... no, not nice ... it is *interesting* to put a face to the name after all these weeks of communicating in secret,' Boris began. 'Untraceable phone calls and coded messages on old sweet wrappers are all well and good, but it is important to know who you are dealing with. I have to admit, however, that you are not what I was expecting. I am sure my brother feels the same.'

'Do not tell me how to feel!' scowled Igor. I stepped back in horror as the more irritable of the Bottle Brothers lunged towards me. Thankfully, all he wanted to do was copy Boris and shake me roughly by the hand. His grip was equally as firm, whilst his smell – cardboard – was just as serious.

'Introductions over,' said Boris. 'Where is it?'

'Where's *what?*' I shrugged.

Igor swapped my hand for my neck as he lifted me up off the ground.

'Your equipment,' explained Boris. 'You told us that you had some of the most advanced vault-cracking equipment in the history of vault-cracking equipment. So, Mr Fox, where is it?'

'*Vault-cracking equipment?*' Suddenly I knew what Wrinkles had stolen from Room *404* and why Silver Fox had been so panic-stricken about it. Without the equipment, the Bottle Brothers would know he was a fraud. That he wasn't a vault-cracker at all, but something else entirely. The *something else* being a spy.

Luckily for Silver Fox, he was no longer the one who would have to deal with the consequences.

No, that was me.

'In case you have forgotten,' said Boris, 'the vault at the Bottle Bank has one of the most securely secure security systems ever invented. Nobody can gain access, except for those who have deposited their fortunes. It is how we designed it. That way it can never be broken into, not even by my brother and I.' Boris paused. '*Until now,*' he said with a sly grin. 'So, I shall ask you again, Mr Fox. Where is your equipment?'

I tried to speak, but found it harder than usual. Igor realised this and dropped me like a hot potato straight from the oven.

'Where's my equipment?' I tapped my forehead whilst I frantically thought of an answer. Eight taps later and I decided that *my forehead* might just be the best answer I could come up with. 'I keep it here,' I said smugly. 'Tucked away where no one can get at it. Thirteen years of vault-cracking experience all wrapped up in one tiny brain.'

Silver Fox had heard enough. Jerking his head from side to side, he made a noise like a choking goat before he spat out the sock. 'Please,' he begged. 'Just let me speak.'

'I don't think that's necessary,' I said, driving the sock back into his mouth.

'You promised we would be alone, Mr Fox.' Boris stopped talking and pointed at Agent One. 'And yet I see we have company.'

'He's not company,' I blurted out. 'I don't even know him. He just happened to be here when I walked in. We should really call the police—'

'No police,' insisted Boris. 'We shall deal with this ... *nearly naked man* ourselves. So, is this how you found him? *In just his underpants? In your hotel room?*'

'That's right,' I nodded.

'And then you tied him to that chair?' pressed Boris.

'That's right,' I nodded again.

'And now you're going to kill him?' said Boris coldly.

'That's ... *wrong!* I cried. '*Very* wrong. I'm not going to kill him!'

'Do you want *me* to kill him?' said Igor, perking up a little.

'No, I do not!' I said. 'Why can't we just ... you know ... threaten him a bit?'

'Threaten him?' Boris removed his glasses and wiped

them on the front of his jacket. 'What would you have us do, Mr Fox? *Pinch him under his armpit? Pull his nose-hairs?*

'That works for me,' I said, relieved.

'Well, it does not work for us,' scowled Boris. 'We have not got where we are today by simply threatening people. No, this nearly naked man knows who we are and what we are planning. There is only one way to eradicate such a problem. Brother, if you would be so kind ...'

'Problem eradication about to commence,' grinned Igor. He placed his briefcase on the carpet and opened it up. My stomach turned at the thought of what horrors lay inside. An axe or machete perhaps. A claw hammer or knuckleduster. A cheese grater or samurai sword ...

Whoa there! Did I just ...?

Yes, I did.

'Watch and learn,' said Igor, as he ran the cheese grater across his fingertips. 'This nearly naked man is about to endure pain beyond his worst nightmares.'

'Wouldn't it be easier if I just fetched some cheese?' I suggested.

'We do not stop for lunch,' insisted Boris. 'Brother, begin ...'

Silver Fox turned to me in despair as Igor knelt down by his feet. I didn't know where to look so I closed my eyes instead. When I opened them (approximately twelve seconds later) Igor had pressed the cheese grater up to the sole of Fox's bare foot and started to rub. He moved gently at first. Nothing too strenuous. Fox wriggled about a bit, but I don't know why. Maybe it tickled.

That all changed, however, when Igor decided to speed things up.

Suddenly Silver Fox's face was twisting and turning in all manner of directions. Behind his mouthful of sock, he was either laughing or screaming. Either way, I had to put a stop to things before they got any worse.

I was all set to make my move when a thin sliver of daylight caught my eye. It was coming from a slight gap in the curtain that ran along the back wall of *404*. Behind the curtain there was a glass window that, up until then, I had failed to notice. And behind the window ...

'Give me that!' I said, snatching the cheese grater from Igor's hand. As I tossed it across the room, I sneaked a quick peek at Silver Fox's foot. It was red raw, but there was no sign of any blood.

'What are you doing?' cried Boris.

'Hurrying things along, that's what,' I replied. 'This *human grating* is so slow it's starting to grate on me.'

Before either Bottle could argue, I wandered over to the curtain and pulled it open.

'Why don't we just leave the nearly naked man out there?' I said, pointing at the balcony that I had spotted outside. 'That'll put a stop to him. Maybe for good if the temperature drops and he freezes solid. What do you think?'

Boris took a moment before answering. 'I think, yes, it is one way of hurrying things along,' he said, eventually. 'Brother, if you would do the honours ...'

I crossed the carpet as Igor picked up both Silver Fox and the chair. Lifting the latch, I slid the window to one side, allowing him to wander straight out onto the balcony. Before I knew it, Igor was back in the room and Silver Fox wasn't. Shivering in just his underpants, I could feel his eyes staring straight at me as I locked the window and closed the curtain on him. He needn't have worried. I had already promised myself that I would come back and get him when I had finished with the Bottles. That would take an hour or two. Three maximum. Despite what I'd said before, there was no way he would freeze in that time.

Well, *probably* no way.

Alright, *hopefully* no way.

Okay, so there was a *way*, but let's not over-analyse things.

'It is time to go,' ordered Boris. 'You have everything you need, yes, Mr Fox?'

'I've got *more* than everything,' I said, tapping my forehead as I made my way towards the door. Unfortunately, the door was no longer attached to its hinges so I had to take a slight detour to the doorway.

The Bottle Brothers were right behind me as I walked out into the corridor. I'm not proud to admit it, but I left Room *404* just how I had found it.

A complete mess.

Minus one nearly naked man and his chair, of course.

13.'THIS IS OUR WAY INTO THE BOTTLE BANK.'

On paper, the journey from the Hard Times Hotel to the Bottle Bank was nothing more than a short stroll.

Paper, however, has probably never had the misfortune of travelling anywhere with two bothersome brothers like Boris and Igor Bottle. The rain may have dried up, but then so too had the conversation. They didn't talk, so I didn't talk. They just growled and grunted. So I just growled and grunted. That's how it was. Not exactly enjoyable (although still preferable to having my feet *grated* like Silver Fox).

Wary of being spotted out in the open, Igor wisely avoided Coco in the hotel lobby and led us out through the fire exit instead. We found ourselves plunged into a myriad of narrow side streets and tight passageways that not only turned an easy journey into an endless one, but also presented complications of their own. Busy pedestrians and heavy traffic were no longer a problem. Now we had to deal with rickety old fences, overgrown weeds and steaming piles of dog poop.

I won't lie; I was fearful for my slippers. And my slippers, in turn, were fearful for me.

'What are you going to do with all the money I steal from your vault?' I blurted out. As questions go it was a little rash, but I had to break the silence somehow. 'Nice hair transplant perhaps? Blonde and curly would suit you both.' I tugged gently on Boris's sleeve. 'Your brother could probably do with a personality transplant,' I whispered.

'He heard that,' said Boris.

'I heard that,' repeated Igor.

'If you insult one Bottle, you insult us all,' said Boris. 'My brother has already informed me that he wishes to throw you in the Crooked Canal when this is over. That, however, depends.'

I didn't like to ask, but that wasn't enough to stop me. 'On what?'

'On how irritating you are,' explained Boris.

'Oh, I can be *really* irritating,' I foolishly admitted.

'Then it is more than likely that, once this is over, you will go swimming with the fishes,' warned Boris. '*Understand?*'

I placed a hand over my mouth to show that I knew a threat when I heard one. Don't get me wrong; I wasn't scared. But I had forgotten my armbands, so it was probably for the best that I stayed on the Bottles' good side (if such a *side* even existed).

Forty-six tedious minutes later we reached our destination. Recycle Row was a cobbled lane with small, stumpy houses on either side. If I squinted hard enough I could just about make out the Bottle Bank in the distance.

All shiny and new and built entirely of glass, it stood out like a sausage at a vegetarian buffet compared to its stony surroundings.

'*Wait!*' Boris stopped suddenly and placed a hand across my chest. As he did so, the electronic door to the Bottle Bank buzzed open and five men and five women, all dressed head-to-toe in regulation brown, appeared on the pavement. The last woman to leave tapped a code into a control panel and the door closed behind her. With the bank safe and secure, she then followed the other nine into the Rotten Egg, a shabby-looking pub across the road.

'It is lunchtime,' said Boris, removing his hand. 'We have an hour before they return.'

'An hour to empty the vault of its contents,' said Igor greedily.

'The vault we were told could never be cracked,' added Boris, scowling at me as he set off again.

'Stop panicking,' I said, hurrying to keep up. 'I'll crack your vault in the blink of an eye. Sometimes I can just flutter my eyelashes and they open.'

The Bottle Brothers exchanged stern glances. There was no way of knowing what they were thinking. Or even if they were thinking at all.

With the Bottle Bank looming closer with every step, I was all set to wander straight up to the front entrance when Boris changed direction and steered me to my right. *The Crumbling Ruin* was written on a plaque above the door of one of the houses (which, as it turns out, was both the house name and a perfectly apt description of the building itself).

'This is not good,' muttered Boris.

'Not good at all,' agreed Igor.

'*Very* not good at all,' I chipped in. 'I mean, what sort of chump would own a dreary old dump like this?'

'Make that two chumps,' said Boris, straight-faced. 'With me being one of them.'

'And me the other,' said Igor. He gestured angrily towards the door. Not only was it riddled with woodworm, but it was also slightly ajar.

'Don't look at me!' I said, although nobody actually was. 'I didn't open it. And even if I did, I doubt even the most desperate of thieves would want to steal anything from this filthy flea-pit.'

Boris shook his head whilst his brother shook my neck.

'I am not concerned about the house.' Lifting his boot, Boris stamped down on the cobbles. 'I am concerned about what lies beneath it,' he said. 'This is our way into the Bottle Bank.'

Before I could speak, Boris opened the door a little wider and Igor threw me inside. By the time I had picked myself up, the Bottles were right behind me. I watched as Igor placed his briefcase amongst the dust and debris and opened it up.

'This isn't the time or place for grating cheese,' I said.

'He knows,' growled Boris.

'I know,' echoed Igor. When he stood up he was carrying a rolling pin instead. '*But it is time for smashing skulls!*'

Fearing the worst, I turned towards the door.

'Not *your* skull,' said Boris, pulling me back by my

father's dressing gown. 'You're safe ... *for now.*'

'Although that may not be the case if you fail to crack our vault,' added Igor, as he set off up the stairs in search of intruders.

That just left me and Boris.

'You haven't done much with the place, have you?' I said. I wasn't being rude; just stating a fact. A fact backed up by squeaky floorboards, bare stone walls and a whole lot of nothing else in every single room.

'This is not our home,' replied Boris testily. 'We only bought it because of our plan to rob the Bottle Bank.'

'*You actually paid money for it?*' I gasped.

'The house was cheap,' admitted Boris, 'but in the long run it will prove invaluable.'

'It is all clear,' said Igor, as he stomped back down the stairs.

'Very good, brother,' nodded Boris. 'Check all the other rooms whilst I keep an eye on Mr Fox.'

'There's really no need,' I said, as Igor barged past me. 'I'm perfectly capable of keeping an eye on myself.'

Boris raised himself onto the tips of his toes so we were eyeball to eyeball. 'There is something about you I do not like.'

'It's the pyjamas, isn't it?' I said. 'Just tell me the truth. I won't be offended.'

'*Brother, come quickly!*'

Boris grabbed my sleeve and dragged me along the hallway as we followed Igor's voice. We found him in another empty room at the back of the house. He was stood over a large hole slap-bang in the middle of the floorboards.

'I did not leave the trapdoor like this,' Igor said.

'And neither did I,' frowned Boris. 'First the door and now this. I have a bad feeling.'

'I have the same bad feeling,' said Igor.

'And I don't really see what all the fuss is about,' I said. Surely all he had to do was close the trapdoor and that would be the end of it. Job done. Nothing to get your knickers in a knot about.

'I think that Mr Fox should go first, brother,' said Igor, with a twisted grin.

'I agree,' nodded Boris.

'And I'm undecided,' I shrugged. 'Largely because I have no idea where you want me to go to.'

Igor pointed into the hole. '*Down.*'

'*Oh.*' I didn't have to think about it for long. 'In that case, I'd rather not,' I said. 'Although something tells me that I don't really have a ... *whoa!*'

Before I could finish my sentence, Igor lifted me up by my ears and dangled me over the open trapdoor. I knew what was about to happen.

He was going to let go of me.

And he did.

14. 'YOU DID IT!'

I hit the ground before I had chance to scream.

It wasn't a long drop, but that's not to say it wasn't painful when I landed. Bottom-first on a huge pile of broken stones and jagged rubble normally is.

'Are you okay, Mr Fox?' shouted Boris, although he didn't seem overly concerned for my well-being.

'Not really,' I grumbled.

'But you are still alive, yes?' said Igor.

'Obviously,' I muttered.

'Then that is all that matters,' said Boris bluntly. 'Next time you should try using the ladder.'

'*Ladder?* What ladder?' I carefully removed my mother's umbrella from where it had lodged itself before using it to push myself up off the ground. I could see both Bottles stood over the trapdoor, staring down at me. They looked almost happy. Maybe they enjoyed seeing me in pain. My mood didn't improve when I spotted the ladder leant up against the wall.

'There are two torches down there,' said Boris. 'One for me and—'

'One for me,' finished Igor.

'And I suppose I'll have to go without,' I moaned.

'That is correct,' said Boris. 'Find the torches and pass them to us. We need to see where we are going.'

I placed the tip of the umbrella on the ground and moved it around in a wide arc in a fairly useless attempt to stumble upon anything that felt remotely like a torch. When that failed, I dropped down on to my hands and knees and began to brush my fingers over the rough stony surface.

'Time is ticking, Mr Fox,' snapped Boris. 'Hurry up.'

'I am hurrying up,' I snapped back. 'If only I had something to help me see better—'

'Like a torch?' suggested Igor.

'Yes, like a ... *oh, very funny.*' For the first time since I had been stuck in the hole, I looked somewhere other than up and down. 'I can see a light in the distance,' I called out. 'What is this place anyway? Some kind of tunnel?'

'Not *some kind of* tunnel!' snarled Boris, his anger rising. 'It is *the* tunnel! The tunnel that we have dug that leads straight to the vault. And, for your information, there should not be a light in the distance because the tunnel is blocked by a fake wall. A fake wall that we built to replace the old wall that we knocked down.'

'Well, I'm only telling you what I can see,' I said. 'Come and look for yourself if you don't believe me.'

Next thing I knew I was knocked clean off my feet as both Bottles appeared in the tunnel beside me.

'Mr Fox is telling the truth,' Igor had to admit. 'The torches have gone. And I, too, can see a light in the distance.

What does it mean, brother?'

'It means you have been very careless,' replied Boris sternly.

'I am not to blame,' growled Igor. 'Say that again and you shall suffer the consequences.'

'You … have … been … very … careless,' said Boris slowly.

It didn't take a genius to see where this was going. As Boris and Igor began to grapple in the darkness, I shifted to one side and then set off towards the light in the distance. The tunnel may have been big enough for your average Bottle to stand up straight in, but I had to bend my knees, arch my back and take the deepest breath imaginable. And even then I could barely squeeze through.

'Come back, Mr Fox!' shouted Boris, mid-scuffle.

I ignored him and kept on moving. With every small, shuffling step, the light increased in size. I tried to focus on it, but soon got distracted by the sound of scampering feet behind me. The Bottle Brothers had clearly decided to stop fighting and catch up with me instead. And, by the look of things, it was a wise decision.

'*The fake wall!*' cried Boris, as we reached the end of the tunnel. '*It has gone!*'

'It hasn't gone far,' I said, pointing at a large pile of bricks by our feet. Where the wall had been there was now a hole large enough for me to climb through.

So that was what I did.

I found myself in a brightly lit room with a low ceiling and thick concrete walls all around me. To my left there was a staircase and to my right a huge circular steel door.

'This is it,' remarked Boris, shoving me to one side. 'The secret basement under the Bottle Bank. And that ...' He gestured towards the steel door. 'That is the vault. That is where we keep all of our customers' valuables.'

'*Let me in!*' Igor followed his brother's lead and pushed past me. 'Where are they?' he growled.

'Panic not,' said Boris. 'There is nobody down here. Only you and I ... *and the stupid boy!*'

'Don't forget about me,' I said. Then I realised he hadn't.

'Now is the moment for you to weave your magic, Mr Fox,' demanded Boris. 'You have five minutes to crack the vault.'

'*Five minutes?*' I said. 'What am I going to do with the extra four minutes and fifty seconds?'

I walked forward and pretended to study the steel door. I had no idea what I was doing, a fact that both Bottles would very soon figure out for themselves if I wasn't careful.

'The vault has been fitted with a wide array of anti-theft devices,' announced Boris proudly.

'Pleased to hear it,' I replied. Now I'm no expert, but it certainly looked like a complex locking system. Much harder than our bathroom door at home and it wasn't unheard of for me to struggle with that.

'There are exactly four hundred and thirty-seven safety-deposit boxes stored inside,' continued Boris. 'Money ... jewels ... antiques ... *are you nearly in yet?*'

'Almost,' I lied. I pressed my ear up to the vault. Then I rubbed my cheek against it. Then, as a last resort, I grabbed the handle. To my amazement, it dropped and the door began to open.

'You did it!' cried Boris. 'You *actually* did it!'

'No, really, I didn't,' I said.

'Astonishing,' gasped Igor, as he hurried towards me. 'I assumed you were completely useless.'

'I am,' I insisted.

'I thought it could not be cracked,' said Boris, patting me firmly on the back.

'Well, not by me it can't,' I said. 'I didn't do anything. The vault was already open.'

Boris stopped patting and clenched his fists instead. 'That cannot be,' he said. 'The vault is never left open. And we are the only people down here.'

I motioned for the Bottles to come closer. As I expected, they completely ignored me. 'What if you're wrong?' I said regardless. 'What if there is somebody else down here?'

'Do not talk nonsense,' spat Igor. 'There's nowhere to hide.'

I pointed at the steel door. 'There is one place to hide,' I whispered. 'What if they're already inside the vault?'

15.'WHAT ARE YOU DOING IN OUR VAULT?'

Igor pulled the door to one side so the three of us could enter the vault.

We may have been stood in a line, but I was already at least seven steps ahead of both Bottles. Seven *mind* steps. Whereas they were none the wiser, I had a feeling I knew exactly what I was looking for.

Or rather, *who*.

The first thing I saw in the vault were hundreds of identical rectangular boxes, all of which had been emptied and then strewn across the floor.

The second thing, however, would never have been stored away for safe keeping.

It was Wrinkles.

She was on her knees, stuffing bank notes, gold bars and huge handfuls of jewellery into her already bulging knitting bag.

'What – is – that?' stuttered Boris.

'I think it's human, but I can't be certain,' I replied. 'Let me introduce you to—... *whoa!*

Igor pressed me up against the wall before I could finish my sentence.

'You know each other!' he spat. 'Are you in this together?'

'We're in the vault together, but that's all,' I insisted. 'We're not friends. Wrinkles hates me. And I hate her. Like an egg hates a whisk. Honestly. Ask her if you don't believe me.'

'Maybe I will.' Igor dropped me without warning and then turned to confront the hooded intruder. 'What are you doing in our vault?' he shouted.

Wrinkles refused to look up as she continued to fill her knitting bag.

'Answer my brother's question,' demanded Boris.

His words, however, fell on deaf ears. With her head down, Wrinkles closed the bag and climbed slowly to her feet. Even with her back hunched she was still taller than both Bottles.

'How dare you try and rob our bank!' snarled Boris.

'Well, you both dared,' I said, picking myself up off the floor. 'You're just annoyed that Wrinkles got here before you.'

I ducked as Igor swung wildly in my direction. At the same time Wrinkles reached into her knitting bag and removed a ball of wool. Or so I thought. I quickly changed my mind when she threw it down and smoke began to rise into the air, blinding me in an instant. I staggered backwards until I found myself outside of the vault. Rushing back in was one option, but it certainly wasn't top of my list.

I could no longer see either Bottle through the thick fog of smoke, but that didn't mean I couldn't hear them.

'Get her, brother!' cried Boris.

'I am trying,' yelled Igor. 'And stop telling me what to … *oof!*'

There was a heavy *thunk*. It sounded familiar. Like a knitting bag crashing against a skull. Right on cue, Igor tumbled out into the basement and didn't get back up again.

From somewhere within the vault I heard a howling roar. I guessed that Boris was charging deeper into the smoke. And deeper into trouble.

Thunk.

Different brother, same result.

Both Bottles were now flat-out by my feet. With no wish to join them, I took another step back as wave upon wave of billowing smoke seeped into the basement. It was coming to get me … *and Wrinkles was right behind it.*

Like a petrified penguin on thin ice, I froze as something sharp emerged from out of the haze and landed on the tip of my nose. It was a knitting needle. Wrinkles was holding it in one hand, whilst her other struggled with the knitting bag. With one big heave, she threw the bag over her shoulder before hopping over both Bottles on her way to the hole in the wall. Then she was gone.

And so was I.

Diving back into the tunnel, I set off in hot pursuit of my wrinkly adversary. With every stride, my forehead cracked against the makeshift ceiling, but it wasn't enough to slow me down. Not at first anyway. It didn't take long, however, before my head was throbbing so much that I would willingly have chopped it off. Thankfully, a light up ahead convinced me otherwise.

It was the trapdoor.

I heard the door to The Crumbling Ruin slam shut as I scrambled up the ladder. There wasn't a second to waste. Wrinkles was faster than she looked and she already had a healthy lead on me.

I hurried through the house, bouncing from wall to wall as I raced towards the door. Before I knew it, I was outside. Wrinkles, however, wasn't. I looked up and down Recycle Row, but she was nowhere to be seen.

Behind me, I heard the urgent squeal of an alarm. It was coming from the Bottle Bank. I tried to ignore it, but only succeeded in hearing something else in the distance. It was the sound of sirens.

The Crooked Constabulary were on their way.

If ever there was a time to flee, it was now. If I was found at the scene of the crime (or, more accurately, stood outside The Crumbling Ruin with its secret tunnel that led directly to the bank's vault), I would instantly become prime suspect number one. And rightly so.

The sound of sirens increased dramatically as four police cars, a fire engine and an ambulance turned onto the cobbles. Covering my head with my father's dressing gown, I walked slowly towards them, my fingers crossed that nobody would stop to ask why I was wandering around in my pyjamas. As luck would have it, every last one of them whizzed straight past, before the sound of screeching brakes seemed to suggest that they had come to a halt outside the Bottle Bank. I could've looked back, but I didn't. I just kept on walking.

Like Wrinkles, it seemed that I had escaped unnoticed.

'*Watch where you're going!*'

With my eyes still glued to the cobbles, I turned the corner at the top of Recycle Row and walked straight into a friendly face. Okay, not exactly friendly, but familiar. Okay, not that familiar, but at least he hadn't tried to kill me in the short time I had known him. Not yet, anyway.

'Did you see her?' I asked.

'*No.*' The postman didn't bother to look up as he removed a large bundle of mail from his postbag. 'Definitely not.'

'You don't even know who I'm talking about,' I said.

'I don't need to,' shrugged the postman. 'I'm far too busy sticking my fingers in letterboxes to notice anything else.'

I reluctantly believed him. Curiously, it seemed to fit with what Coco had said back at the Hard Times Hotel. She hadn't seen Wrinkles either. It didn't make sense, but then I was starting to learn that not much ever did in the life of a spy.

'I've got a letter for you, Master Hugo Dare,' said the postman, passing me an envelope. 'Or should that be … *Pink Weasel?*'

'How did you know where I'd be?' I asked.

'I read the address,' frowned the postman. 'I do that a lot in my job.'

I looked down at the envelope. Sure enough, the address did kind of give it away.

Pink Weasel,
Just up from The Crumbling Ruin,
Recycle Row,
Crooked Elbow.

I ripped open the envelope and removed the slip of paper inside. The message, like before, was short and to the point.

Come to the SICK Bucket.
NOW.
You're already ten minutes late.
The Big Cheese.
P.S. Make that eleven minutes.
P.P.S. Bring a spade.

The postman tapped me on the shoulder. 'That message will set alight in five—'

I slipped the paper onto my tongue and swallowed it before he could say another word. A moment later I felt the same burning sensation rising in my chest before I burped and a plume of smoke came out of my mouth. To my surprise, the postman looked far from impressed as I showed him my tongue.

'May I offer you a word of advice?' he said, suddenly serious. 'Be careful out there. The streets of Crooked Elbow aren't as safe as you might think.'

'That's the understatement of the century!' I blurted out. 'Almost everyone I've met today has tried to hurt me in some way or another.'

'You'd better get used to it,' said the postman matter-of-factly. 'Some people have murder in mind.'

I was about to ask him what he meant when my attention was drawn to events behind me. Recycle Row was alive with noise and confusion as the police dragged the Bottle Brothers out of their bank and onto the cobbles. Wary of being spotted, I turned to leave, shocked to find that the postman had already beaten me to it. I didn't take it personally.

He had things to do.

And so did I.

Although according to the Big Cheese, I was already eleven minutes late to *do them*.

16.'YOU'RE OUT OF YOUR DEPTH!'

I arrived at The Impossible Pizza exactly twenty-four minutes after I had left Recycle Row.

Mindful of the time, I half-ran, half-skipped there, but it was still much later than the *NOW* that the Big Cheese had requested. My plan was to ignore Impossible Rita as I slipped quietly onto the premises, but she had no intention of ignoring me. Fortunately, she stopped short of a full-on assault and chose, instead, to simply tweak my ear. It hurt a little, but not enough to prevent me from sliding down the rubbish chute straight into the arms of the waiting Rumble. Just like that morning, he gave me one of his special *cuddles* before sending me silently on my way.

With my body aching all over from events at the Bottle Bank, I gazed longingly at the lavatory as I hurried through the SICK Bucket. Surely the life of a toilet boy couldn't be as challenging as that of a spy. Yes, it probably had its moments, but nothing that a nose-peg and an industrial-strength scrubbing brush couldn't conquer.

'Afternoon, Miss Finefellow.' With her eyes glued to a holiday brochure, the Big Cheese's secretary refused to look up as I stopped at her desk. 'Going away?' I asked.

'I was hoping *you* might,' Finefellow muttered. 'You're not really cut out to be a spy, are you, Dare? The robbery at the Bottle Bank was an absolute disaster. Not only did you know what the Bottle Brothers were planning to do, but you helped them do it! You're out of your depth!'

'Then maybe you could save me before I drown,' I said smoothly. 'In fact, leave me too long and I might just need a spot of mouth-to-mouth.'

'That's not going to happen,' said Finefellow bluntly. 'Not today. Not tomorrow—'

'But maybe the day after,' I said, interrupting her. 'This is nice, isn't it? Us getting to know each other a little better. The thing is, I really have to—'

'*Go!*' said Finefellow. At the same time, she lifted the brochure so that it covered her entire face. Call me a fool in love, but it seemed that the ice maiden was finally warming to my charms. All I needed now was a flame thrower and she'd be like water in my hands.

Reluctantly, I left Finefellow where I had found her and sauntered over to the Pantry door. I knocked once, blinked twice and then burst in without an invite.

'Get out!' boomed the Big Cheese. Sat behind a huge pile of boxes, he was doing what he did best. Tucking into a slice of pizza.

'You asked to see me, sir,' I said.

'Did I?' The Big Cheese stopped mid-chew. 'Who are you exactly?'

'I'm exactly Hugo Dare,' I said.

'Hugo Dare?' bawled the Big Cheese. 'Don't be ridiculous! Young Dare is a little scab of a boy. He's so feeble he can barely open his mouth.' The Big Cheese stopped to look me up and down. 'In hindsight, you are quite similar,' he had to admit. 'Almost identical, in fact. Okay, I'll take your word for it. I'm sorry for any misunderstanding, young Dare. I've had a lot on my plate.'

'I didn't know you bothered with a plate, sir,' I said. 'I thought you just ate it straight out the box.'

'Needs must,' mumbled the Big Cheese, as he stuffed more pizza into his mouth. 'And, plate or no plate, when I need to eat, I must. Talking of which, would you care for some? It's my favourite. Avocado and anchovies. It's a pizza for real spies. Puts hairs on your tongue and everything.'

He tossed me a slice, but I missed it and it splattered against the wall.

'Not to worry,' said the Big Cheese. 'There's plenty more where that came from ... *just not for you!* Right, let's talk spy, shall we? I'll be honest, young Dare, after what happened at the Bottle Bank I wasn't expecting to see you back here quite so ... *alive.* You're not a ghost, are you?'

'Not that I'm aware of, sir,' I said. 'It'll take more than a pair of bungling Bottles to finish me off.'

'That's a shame,' grumbled the Big Cheese. 'Because if you were a ghost then that would probably explain why you failed so badly. Silver Fox has told me everything. You do remember Silver Fox, don't you?'

I screwed up my face. 'Yes ... well ... I do now,' I said

awkwardly. 'Which reminds me, there's somewhere I need to be.'

'Not any more there's not,' said the Big Cheese firmly. 'Don't ask me how he did it, but Fox managed somehow to free himself from the chair and climb down the balcony. He told me that you pretended to be a vault-cracker and then joined the Bottle Brothers in trying to rob their own bank. If Fox hadn't called the police they would probably have got away with it, too. Although that doesn't explain why all the valuables from the vault still seem to have mysteriously disappeared.'

'That's no mystery, sir,' I said. 'I blame Wrinkles.'

'*Wrinkles? At your age?*' The Big Cheese rolled his eyes. 'I've heard some excuses in my time, but that takes the biscuit.'

'Wrinkles is a woman, sir,' I explained. 'Or a crazy old crab-stick to be precise. It was her who robbed the Bottle Bank. And she managed to do it because she knew everything we were about to do and then did it first.'

'That's not possible,' said the Big Cheese. 'Not unless …' He stopped to pull on his moustache. 'Not unless we have a mole here in the SICK Bucket,' he said under his breath.

'*A mole?*' I was stood on my chair before the words had even left my lips. 'Why don't you just put it back in your garden where it belongs?'

'Not that kind of mole, you blithering bunion,' roared the Big Cheese. 'In spy terms, a mole is someone who's been sent to pose as an agent so they can penetrate an organisation – in this case SICK – and then pass on top-secret intelligence to the enemy – as in your wrinkly old thief.'

'Yes, that sounds about right,' I said.

'To you it might,' blasted the Big Cheese, 'but to me it sounds like a stinking pile of cow dung! Like it or not, young Dare, you're tinkling up the wrong lamppost.'

'I didn't know I was tinkling up *any* lamppost!' I insisted. 'But I am right when I say that Wrinkles was always one step ahead of me this morning. She knew about the Hard Times Hotel and where to find Silver Fox. She knew how he had fooled the Bottle Brothers into thinking that he was a vault-cracker and that he had the equipment to prove it. And she even knew about The Crumbling Ruin and its secret tunnel that leads directly into the bank's basement—'

'Coincidence … coincidence … coincidence.' It was no coincidence that I found the Big Cheese very irritating when he said this. 'Your imagination is out of control, young Dare,' he continued. 'There are lots of wrinkly grandmas roaming the streets of Crooked Elbow, covered in cat hair, tripping you up with their shopping baskets, but not one of them has the skills or the expertise to do all the things you've mentioned. No, the only person with grey hair I'm worried about is Silver Fox. Nothing's changed since this morning's debacle. Fox has already gone back out undercover and I still need you to assist him.'

'I'm all ears, sir,' I said. 'Well, not *all* ears because that would be no use to anybody. Especially not Silver Fox, who's got two perfectly good ears of his own.' I took a breath. 'Just tell me what I need to know please, sir.'

'For some time now, SICK have suspected upper-crust

criminal family, the Majestic Mob, of smuggling jewels into Crooked Elbow through the Crooked Canal,' the Big Cheese began. 'Unfortunately, we've never been able to catch them at it. *Until now.* The canal has burst its banks and the Majestics have been forced to find a new route. A route that we believe passes straight through the Pearly Gates Cemetery. Silver Fox is there now. As well as posing as a vault-cracker, he's also been working deep undercover as a gravedigger. That's what you'll be doing, too. Father O'Garble is expecting you even as we speak. Now, your instructions, young Dare, are so simple that even a baby could understand them.'

'Would you like me to fetch one, sir?' I said.

'*Never!*' boomed the Big Cheese. 'Babies and SICK do not go well together. No, all I want you to do is find Fox and then stay close to him. Nothing more, nothing less.' The Big Cheese hesitated. 'You did bring a spade, didn't you?'

I screwed up my face. 'A spade, sir?'

'Those were my instructions,' said the Big Cheese. 'Every gravedigger needs a spade.'

'In that case … *yes, I did,*' I lied.

'Good,' nodded the Big Cheese. 'Where is it?'

'It's … *hidden,*' I lied again. 'Inside my pyjamas. It's quite a snug fit, but I can always—'

'Leave it where it is,' said the Big Cheese, finishing my sentence. 'Good hiding place, though. Right, take that spade, young Dare – and whatever else you might have hidden about your person – and get out of my sight. And no more talk of wrinkly wrongdoers.'

'But, sir—' I began.

'No *buts*,' said the Big Cheese. 'Or *ifs*. Or *maybes*. There's only so many mistakes an agent can make … and you've made all of yours in one morning! Miss Finefellow has already called you the worst spy she's ever known.'

'At least she called me a spy,' I said smugly. 'Think about it. She could've called me the worst *person* she's ever known. Still, it's up to me to prove her wrong. And I will do. From now on, I'll be at the top of my game, sir. I won't stop until I've made you proud. Not even to go to the lavatory.'

'You'll need a strong bladder,' sighed the Big Cheese, as he grabbed another slice of pizza.

'The strongest,' I said. With that, I patted my pelvis before sweeping out of the Pantry.

Destination the Pearly Gates Cemetery.

There was a gravedigger I had to get together with.

17.'LEAVING SO SOON?'

The first thing I did when I left the Pantry was nip to the lavatory.

Nerves, I guess. Then I exited the SICK Bucket via The Impossible Pizza and headed straight for the Pearly Gates Cemetery.

Well, almost *straight*. Straight with a slight bend.

A slight bend to pick up a spade.

It was mid-afternoon by the time I arrived back home. As number thirteen Everyday Avenue came into view, I caught sight of a familiar flash of orange lurking by the door. It was my mother. And she didn't seem particularly happy to see me.

'Really, Doreen,' I said, 'I know I've been gone all morning, but there's no need to look so worried.'

'It's not worry, dear,' Doreen frowned. 'It's disappointment. Disappointment that you've come home at all. For one joyful moment, I thought you'd gone and found yourself a proper job. Like on an oil rig.'

'I'm only thirteen,' I reminded her. 'I don't think they'd let me work on an oil rig.'

'More's the pity,' muttered Doreen. 'Although, If I'm being honest, dear, I'm not really surprised that you've come home. Mr Big Cheese called and said you were–'

'The Big Cheese called here?' I blurted out. 'And you spoke to him?'

'Of course I spoke to him,' said Doreen. 'I thought even you understood the workings of a telephone by now.'

'What did he say?' I spluttered.

'He told me you were coming to collect a spade,' revealed Doreen. 'It all sounds a bit silly if you ask me, but if it gets you out of that shed—'

'*Shedroom*,' I said, correcting her. I wasn't concerned that the Big Cheese didn't believe my story about the spade being inside my pyjamas, however plausible it seemed at the time. No, what bothered me most was that he had spoken to my mother. The strangest woman in the whole of Crooked Elbow. My reputation as a spy – if I had one – was surely now in tatters.

I was all set to leave Doreen to her doorstep dusting (or whatever it was she was actually doing) when my mind was struck by a sudden thought. 'If you're not waiting for me, who are you waiting for?' I asked.

'Your father, dear,' sighed Doreen. 'I've not seen him all day. I thought you were him because of that dressing gown, but then I realised that not even Dirk Dare would be daft enough to go out dressed like that. When – or if – he finally decides to come home I'm going to trap his head in the letterbox.'

'Good idea,' I said, humouring her. 'Although have you

ever considered that he might be involved in some top-secret mission?'

'It's an interesting theory, dear,' sniggered Doreen, 'but then how many tea boys do you know that are involved in top-secret missions?'

She had a point, although I would never have admitted it out loud. Instead, I slipped past her and entered the house. Seventeen strides later I had exited through the back door and was halfway across the garden. I had almost reached my shedroom when my armpit erupted into a series of violent spasms. Reaching inside my dressing gown, I pulled out my phone and answered on the fourth vibration.

'*We meet again, Ugo Dayer.*'

I stopped dead in my slippers as the parts of a very simple puzzle (recommended age 3-5 years) slotted worryingly into place. All of a sudden, the postman's advice at the top of Recycle Row made perfect sense. *Some people have murder in mind.* At the time I thought it was just the vague, incoherent ramblings of a man who spent far too much time stroking his letters, but I was wrong.

He wasn't talking about murder.

He was talking about Murder.

My shedroom-shooting sniper from that morning. And, along with Wrinkles, arguably the most dangerous person I'd ever had the misfortune to encounter.

'Are we meeting again?' I asked, hurrying across the garden. 'Yes, you tried to shoot me, and, yes, you also tried to crush me under a crate of milk bottles, but I can't say that we've ever been properly introduced.'

'That may be about to change,' said Murder.

I dived inside my shedroom and shut the door behind me. Okay, so it wasn't the best of hiding places, but it was still preferable to being out in the open. Stood out there, in the middle of the garden, I was an easy target for Murder to shoot at.

'Where are you?' I asked.

'Close,' replied Murder.

I crouched down and peeked through the keyhole. 'How close?'

'*I know where you is* close,' said Murder.

'*Really?* I didn't think anybody knew I'd gone to work on an oil rig,' I said, trying to fool him.

'That is because you have not,' said Murder, proving himself to be less of a fool than I'd hoped. 'No, I think the time has come. The time when I finally introduce myself.'

There was a moments silence before one of the wooden floorboards behind me let out an unnerving *creak*.

'You're in my shedroom, aren't you?' I said nervously.

'Yes, I is,' whispered Murder in my ear.

I felt two hands on my shoulders as I slowly stood up. It left me with no other choice.

Secrets of a Spy Number 30 – if you have to fight, fight dirty.

Spinning around on the spot, I tried to take in as much as I could in a short space of time. Just like that morning, Murder was dressed in black with a balaclava pulled down over his face. The balaclava restricted his view. Which gave me an idea.

As Murder lunged towards me, I raised both my hands

and waved them on either side of his head. Just like I hoped, he turned, distracted, leaving me free to lift my slipper and stamp down on his foot.

I didn't expect it to break any bones (it probably wouldn't even crack a toenail), but Murder still screamed out loud before doubling up in agony. Right there and then, I could've made a run for it.

But what was the point?

Running away would only prolong the inevitable. The inevitable being the moment that Murder decided to come back and try again for a third time. No, one way or another, this had to end.

I knew one way ... *but chose another.*

Grabbing an empty plant pot, I took aim and smashed it over the back of Murder's head. The force was enough to send him crashing through the shedroom door, his hands clutching his balaclava as he staggered out into the open.

'Leaving so soon?' With the lawnmower leading the way, I shot off after him. Murder took one look at the pair of us and ran towards the fence at the foot of the garden. He got there first and scrambled up the wooden panels before eventually disappearing over the other side. I let go of the lawnmower and was about to tackle the fence myself when I heard the grumble of a car engine.

No, it wasn't a car.

My suspicions were proved correct when I peeked through a crack in the fence. There was a milk float trundling along the road. Like before, Murder had made his escape. Unlike before, however, he had left as a broken man, hopefully never to return again.

Without missing a beat, I put the lawnmower back where I had found it, grabbed the spade and closed the shedroom door behind me.

'What was all the noise about, dear?' asked Doreen, as I appeared on the doorstep beside her.

'Just a spot of weeding,' I said. 'Well, one weed in particular, but I don't think we'll be seeing him again anytime soon.'

'That's nice, dear,' said Doreen, barely listening. 'Stay out of trouble, won't you?'

'Probably not,' I said, as I set off along Everyday Avenue.

I wasn't joking.

If today had taught me anything it was that I couldn't avoid trouble ... *and trouble certainly had no intention of avoiding me.*

18. 'AGENT MINUS THIRTY-FIVE TO THE RESCUE.'

It was late afternoon when I finally found myself outside the Pearly Gates Cemetery.

Daylight was fading fast, only to be replaced by a thick layer of fog and an icy chill in the air that was cold enough to make my toenails shiver. Not one to be beaten by the weather, I pulled my pyjama bottoms up past my waist and pressed on into the gloom.

The gates to the cemetery were made of wrought iron and, perhaps most important of all, wide apart. It was an open invitation for me to enter. Which got me thinking.

Secrets of a Spy Number 33 – if it looks like a trap then it most probably is a trap.

Fearing the worst, I avoided the gates and veered, instead, towards a tall brick wall to my left. I tossed my spade over first and then set about scrambling up it the best I could. By the time I had made it over, my fingers were shredded and I had cuts and scratches all over my legs. Still, better that than walk willingly into a trap. If there *was* a trap. Which, if I'm being honest, there probably wasn't. Meaning that all of the above was a complete waste of time.

With my search sensors set to Silver Fox, I made my way along a path that ran the length of the cemetery grounds. Most of the graves I passed were larger than life, although the odd one was small and tucked away. Some were ancient and ugly, whilst others were brand-spanking new and yet somehow even uglier. On the face of it, they weren't that dissimilar to many of my teachers at Crooked Comp'. Nearly all of them were uncared for and in need of a good scrub. That's the graves. Not the teachers. Although, come to think of it ...

I came to a halt at the same time as the path. As far as I could tell the cemetery seemed to be completely deserted. Turning around, I was all set to head back the same way I had just come when I spied a hearse at the gates. Unlike me, it had no fears about driving straight through. Behind it there was a row of sleek black cars. A funeral procession if ever I saw one.

Secrets of a Spy Number 91 – it is better to hide without thinking than to think about hiding.

With that in mind, I dived for cover behind the nearest gravestone I could find. It was made of marble and shaped like an angel. The perfect hiding place for me and my spade.

I peeked out from behind a wing as the hearse trundled slowly through the grounds of the cemetery. The other cars followed close behind. There were six of them in total. Driving bumper to bumper, they were all spotlessly clean with blacked out windows. There was a wooden coffin in the back of the hearse with a large flowery wreath on top. The wreath spelt out one word.

DIAMONDS.

My attention switched from the cars to an elderly man who seemed to have appeared from nowhere. He had straggly white hair that covered much of his face and a long white dress that stretched all the way down to his feet.

I guessed that this was Father O'Garble.

The hearse came to a halt and an impossibly tall man in a top hat, dark suit and knee-high leather boots climbed out of the passenger seat. He joined Father O'Garble and the two of them began to talk.

But not for long.

Stopping mid-sentence, Top Hat reached into the hearse and removed a hooked wooden cane which he used to point at something. I squinted into the fog and realised he was pointing at the angel gravestone.

My angel gravestone!

I had been spotted and I had to get out of there. Fortunately, my body figured this out at the same time as my brain and, before I knew it, I was scurrying backwards at such a speed that my knees barely touched the grass beneath me.

And then I was scurrying no more.

I was falling.

The muddy landing would've been softer if my spade hadn't got there first. That was painful to say the least. To say the most it was *very* painful and I would probably require a hospital visit to remove it.

The mud I was now cuddling up to belonged to a deep, rectangular-shaped hole in the ground. I was all set to climb out when I heard a noise behind me. A sort of muffled cry; it wasn't that dissimilar to a noise I had heard that morning in the Hard Times Hotel.

I turned around and there he was. Agent One. Also known as Silver Fox. Gagged, bound and blindfolded.

And wearing nothing but his underpants.

I crouched down and pulled the gag – the same thick black sock – from out of his mouth.

'Who's there?' cried a panic-stricken Fox.

'Not who – *Hugo*,' I said, removing his blindfold. 'It's me. Pink Weasel. Agent Minus Thirty-Five to the rescue.'

'What are you doing here?' whispered Fox angrily. Yes, I know what you're thinking. Is it even possible to whisper angrily? Surely it's a bit like crying happily. Or snoring tunefully. Or farting fragrantly. Or ... 'I told the Big Cheese I never wanted to see you again,' said Fox, interrupting my stream of thought.

'I'm not that bad,' I said, as I freed his hands. 'In fact, I'm the exact opposite. Although that would just be *not that good*, wouldn't it? And I am. Good, I mean. I'm brilliant. You'll find that out for yourself soon enough. We could be the best of friends in a day or two—'

Fox stuck a hand over my mouth. There was a thick layer of mud under his fingernails, not to mention the remains of several dead insects. 'I don't know why you're here,' he began, 'and, believe me, I wish you weren't, but you need to leave as soon as possible.'

I moved his hand and licked my lips before speaking. 'Ah, that's the problem,' I said. '*It's not.*'

'It's not *what?*' frowned Fox.

'It's not possible,' I explained. 'I'm the new gravedigger. I'm ... *erm* ... here to dig graves. Just like you. Although I'm guessing you've not done much digging recently. Not unless you like working in just your underpants.'

Fox's nose twitched and a sprinkling of dirt fell from his nostrils. 'She was here,' he said, trembling as he spoke. 'That old woman.'

My anger rose as I spat out the name I had made up for her. '*Wrinkles?*'

Fox nodded. 'She caught me unawares. Before I could stop her she had removed my clothes and tied me up—'

'*Again,*' I said. 'Why do you keep on letting that happen? No, don't answer that. We all do peculiar things from time to time. I once munched by way through an entire bowl of dog food. By accident, I might add. Although, when I say once what I really mean is for an entire week. And when I say by accident, I actually mean on purpose. I blame Doreen. There was nothing else to eat. The strange thing is, we haven't even got a dog.'

'Pass me my clothes,' demanded Fox. He pointed over my shoulder at a pile behind me. 'The Majestic Mob will be here at any moment.'

'Or just *this moment,*' I said, handing him his jacket. 'I think they're here already.'

Fox sank back down into the mud. 'Then we're too late,' he sighed.

I was about to agree when a large shadowy figure appeared at the side of the hole. It was Top Hat from the hearse. Up close, he posed a quite formidable figure. His skin was pale, his eyes were black and there was a deep scar running across the length of his neck.

'This is something of a surprise,' he said. For somebody so intimidating, his voice was surprisingly light. 'Allow me to introduce myself. My name is Marmaduke Archibald Pomegranate Majestic The Third, although Duke will suffice. My family and I are here for a funeral.'

'I'm sorry to hear that,' I said.

'Don't be,' said Duke, twirling his cane as he spoke. 'I always find funerals to be unexpectedly enjoyable. Although this one does have its own set of curious complications.'

'Oh, that's a shame,' I said. 'Is it anything I can help you with?'

'I hope so.' Duke jabbed the cane, first at me and then at Silver Fox, who was trying desperately to pull on his clothes. 'You two are in the grave,' he hissed. 'And if you don't get out soon that's where you'll remain for the rest of your loathsome lives!'

19. 'A GOOD SPY NEVER GETS BORED.'

A grave.

Of course it was. Obvious really when you think about it. A rectangular hole dug into the earth in the middle of the Pearly Gates Cemetery.

What else could it be?

'My name is Pink Weasel,' I said, thrusting my hand out. 'But you can call me Pinky.'

A furious-looking Duke Majestic chose not to shake me by the hand. I could hardly blame him. He didn't know where it had been (and neither would he want to).

'He's with me,' said Fox, clambering out of the grave with his jeans around his ankles. 'He's the new gravedigger.'

'I've even got the spade to prove it,' I said, waving the tool above my head.

'A gravedigger?' Duke eyed me suspiciously. 'If that's the case then why has Father O'Garble no idea who he is?'

'Father O'Garble has no idea who his own wife is!' remarked Fox. 'He's as drunk as a skunk for half the day and then completely blotto the rest of it!'

'He's just a boy,' frowned Duke.

'*A boy?*' I said, shocked. 'But he looks so old. Especially with all that white hair.'

'No, *you're* just a boy – not Father O'Garble!' scowled Duke. 'Why aren't you at school?'

'It's the weekend,' I said. 'Although, if I'm being honest, there's not really much more for me to learn. I'm not one to brag, but I was digging graves before people had even figured out how to die.'

'That's ridiculous!' sneered Duke. 'No … *you're* ridiculous! Do you always wear pyjamas to work?'

'Now who's being ridiculous?' I laughed. 'Of course I don't! Sometimes I wear swimming trunks. Especially when it's raining.'

Duke took a breath. 'There is something about you, Weasel, that concerns me. I'm not convinced you are who you say you are.'

'Well, I'm not convinced you are who I say I am either,' I replied.

Duke glared at me. Then Silver Fox glared at me too. Fortunately, I can spot a glare a mile off. Unfortunately, I wasn't so quick to spot Duke as he hooked his cane under the cord of my dressing gown and dragged me out of the grave.

Back on damp grass, the first thing I saw was a group of stern-looking mourners gathered around me. Four of them were carrying the coffin with the floral wreath on top.

'Is … there a … problem?' slurred Father O'Garble, as

he emerged through the crowd.

'There was,' replied Duke, 'but he's just about to disappear.'

'Yes, he's just about to disappear.' I peered up at the leader of the Majestic Mob and realised he was talking about me. 'Okay, have it your way,' I shrugged. 'It's just a shame I couldn't get to say goodbye to the sadly departed Mr Diamonds,' I said, pointing at the wreath. 'Popular, was he?'

'*Popular?*' Duke's top lip curled up into something that almost resembled a smile. 'Words cannot possibly explain how much we all love Shiny Diamonds. Oh, it seems we have company.'

I looked beyond the mourners just in time to see a line of police cars pull up outside the cemetery gates. 'Friends of yours?' I asked.

'I prefer to think of them as unwelcome onlookers ... much like your good self,' said Duke. 'Now, the way I see it, gravedigger, you've got two choices. You can either leave now and forget about everything you've seen, or you can forget about everything you've seen and leave now. Which is it to be?'

'I could always forget to leave whilst remembering everything I haven't seen yet,' I said, confusing even myself.

My teeth clattered together as Duke pushed the cane under my chin.

'Ignore him,' said Fox, stepping between us. 'He's just trying to be funny.'

'I wasn't trying,' I argued. 'I *am* funny. And if you want me to leave, you only have to ask. I can go and dig a hole over there if you like. At the other end of the cemetery. Where you can't see me.'

'Yes, you do that,' Duke sneered.

'I already have.' Carefully side-stepping the open grave in case I fell in for a second time, I set off for *over there*. I could feel dirt in my slippers and something slimy crawling around inside my pyjama bottoms, but neither were uncomfortable enough to make me stop and investigate.

Forty-three paces later I came to a halt and started to dig. The grass was wet from the rain, but the ground underneath was as hard as seaside rock. Every time I pushed the spade down it bounced back and hit me in the face. Thankfully, nobody saw me do it. Not even Silver Fox, who seemed to have done a disappearing act of his own.

Behind me, Father O'Garble began to mumble a few words as the coffin was lowered into the grave. Whatever he said, it seemed to have the desired effect. One by one, the women dabbed at their eyes with tissues, whilst the men bowed their heads as a mark of respect.

Yes, from a distance it looked like any other funeral.

And yet something didn't quite add up. I looked a little closer and saw that some of the mourners were actually smiling. Now, I had never met Shiny Diamonds, but he would have to be one unpopular fellow for people to be enjoying themselves so much whilst at his funeral. And unpopular was one thing he certainly wasn't. Not according to Duke Majestic, anyway.

Fearful of being spotted doing absolutely nothing, I tossed my spade to one side and began to pull the grass out blade by blade with my bare hands. That was when I felt something soft splatter against the side of my face. I wiped it off with my fingers and examined what it left behind.

Mud.

Now I had to find out who had flicked it at me.

My eyes panned across the grounds of the cemetery before finally resting on the hearse. One of the windows had been wound down. If I looked hard enough I could just about make out the outline of a figure sat low in the driver's seat.

It was Fox. And he was beckoning me to join him.

With my spade tucked inside my dressing gown, I dropped onto my stomach and began to slither through the grass. I held my breath as I passed the grave of Shiny Diamonds, but I needn't have worried. The Majestic Mob were far too caught up in the funeral to even notice me, never mind wonder what I was up to.

I carefully opened the door when I reached the hearse and climbed inside. 'Comfortable?' I asked.

'Not particularly,' Fox grumbled. He was sat lower than I had imagined. So low, in fact, that his knees were pressed against his earlobes. 'I don't want them to see me,' he said. 'And I definitely don't want them to see you. Duke Majestic doesn't seem to like you very much.'

'He's not the first,' I shrugged.

'But he might be the last!' warned Fox. He nodded towards the mourners. 'Do you know the one thing that every member of the Majestic Mob has in common?'

I took a moment to think. 'Have they all played the

bagpipes whilst dressed as a monkey at the top of a lighthouse?'

'No … I mean … I don't think … *how am I supposed to know?*' cried Fox. 'No, the one thing they all have in common is that they're not really here for a funeral.'

'Well, that's where you're wrong,' I argued. 'They're here for Shiny Diamonds. He was extremely popular.'

'Shiny Diamonds?' Fox rolled his eyes in despair. 'Shiny Diamonds can't be dead!'

'Shiny Diamonds isn't dead?' I blurted out. 'Then what are we waiting for? Let's break him out of that coffin before it's too late!'

I had opened the door and was halfway out of the hearse before Fox pulled me back inside.

'There's no need to rescue anyone,' he said. 'Shiny Diamonds isn't a person. Shiny Diamonds is just *that*. Lots and lots of very small, very expensive diamonds. The Majestic Mob have been smuggling them into the Pearly Gates ever since they stopped using the Crooked Canal. It's all to do with the coffin.'

'Would you like a glass of water?' I said. 'It'll help to clear your throat—'

'Coffin – not coughing!' groaned Fox. 'The Majestic Mob use empty coffins to smuggle diamonds into Crooked Elbow. They fake a funeral and bury the coffin in the ground. Then, when Father O'Garble has gone to bed and the police are nowhere to be seen, they come back and dig it up. From what I've learnt these fake funerals have been going on every day for the past month.'

'*Wow!* That's a lot of fake tears,' I said.

'No, that's a lot of *real* diamonds,' remarked Fox. 'That's why it has to stop. My plan was to come back tonight and dig up the coffin that they're burying now—'

'*Was?*' I queried.

'Yes ... but then you came along,' confessed Fox.

'Oh, I get it.' I turned and winked at Agent One. 'Okay, I accept.'

'There's nothing to accept,' insisted Fox.

'I accept your invitation,' I said. 'We can dig up the coffin together.'

'That's not what I meant,' said Fox. 'I think I'd rather do it when you're not ... *down!*'

I hit the grass hard as Silver Fox bundled me out of the hearse. The funeral was over. The coffin had been buried, Father O'Garble had finished his rambling sermon and, one by one, the Majestic Mob were beginning to slowly disperse.

'Okay, we'll dig it up together,' whispered Fox, once we'd crawled for cover behind the nearest gravestone. 'The Majestic Mob will be back at midnight so we'll have to get there first. One hour earlier should do the trick.'

I nodded in agreement. 'Ten o'clock?'

'No, eleven,' frowned Fox.

'Even better,' I said.

I looked out from behind the gravestone just in time to see the last of the mourning Majestics climb into their vehicles and depart the Pearly Gates. The police let them pass before following close behind. Only Father O'Garble remained, his straggly white hair slipping even further over his eyes as he wandered aimlessly between the gravestones.

'That's my cue to leave,' said Fox, jumping to his feet. 'There's plenty of time to rest and recover before I come back later ... *at eleven.*' Fox paused. 'You could always go home, too,' he suggested. 'To your own home, I mean. Not mine. In fact, maybe you could stay there and not come back at all. You do understand what I'm saying, don't you?'

'Of course I don't,' I said honestly, 'but I do know that if I stay here at the cemetery I can keep an eye on that coffin. Maybe two eyes if I'm feeling generous.'

'It's your choice,' shrugged Fox. 'Don't blame me if you get bored, though.'

'A good spy never gets bored,' I said smugly.

'And what would you know about that?' said Fox, turning to leave. I gave him a little wave and then tried to get comfortable. Resting my head against the gravestone, I closed my eyes and let my mind drift. If Silver Fox was right, I had a little over six hours to wait until we could snatch the buried bounty from those unsuspecting Majestics. The thought of it reminded me of an old joke I had never heard.

How many mobsters does it take to dig up a coffin?

I was fast asleep before I could even think of the punchline.

20.'YOU ARE UNDER ARREST!'

Two.

That's the punchline to the joke. It's not even funny. And neither was the fact that it was darker than dark when I finally woke up. I knew this because I couldn't see a thing. Not even when I opened my eyes. Still, whether I liked it or not (and I was currently undecided), night-time had reared its murky head and there were no lights anywhere in the Pearly Gates Cemetery to pretend it hadn't.

'*Nice sleep?*'

Ah, I wasn't expecting that. I had company. Not Silver Fox, but a man, nevertheless. I could tell by the voice. It was slow and slurred and vaguely recognisable. I could also tell that he was close. Not *sat-on-my-lap* close, but close enough for me to touch. That's if I wanted to. Which I didn't.

'I wasn't asleep.' Reaching up, I stretched my arms above the gravestone until my elbows clicked back into place. 'I was just in the zone,' I said, yawning. 'Preserving energy. Waiting to be turned on. A bit like a laptop.'

'When it's in sleep mode,' chuckled the man. 'Which is how you've been for a very long time now. I should know. I have been watching you, after all.'

'That doesn't sound very creepy,' I said, shifting nervously on the spot. I blinked several times until my eyes began to adjust to the darkness. The first thing I saw was straggly white hair and a long dress.

'Do you always do that?' asked Father O'Garble.

Unknowingly, I had started to nibble on my fingernails. Then suck on my fingers. Then lick my own palms.

'I'm just hungry,' I said, my stomach rumbling to prove the point. 'I've missed every mealtime going today.'

'Maybe this will help.' O'Garble held out his hand, passing me what, at first, appeared to be a rather large chocolate.

'Is it edible?' I asked.

'I'm not entirely sure,' admitted O'Garble.

'*That's good enough for me.*' With that, I popped it into my mouth, my cheeks bulging as I tried to bite into it. 'Where did you get it?' I mumbled.

'I found it on a dead body,' O'Garble revealed. 'A big lump of a man with black teeth and horrendous breath. He had it lodged in his throat. I may even have been what killed him—'

I tried to spit it out, but only succeeded in swallowing it by accident. Despite its size, it slipped down a treat, resting with a *plop* in the pit of my empty stomach.

'Right, this has been anything but pleasant,' I said, pushing myself up off the ground, 'but there's somewhere I have to be.'

'Me too,' said O'Garble. As I stood up, he sat down. Curiously, he chose the exact same spot that I had only just vacated.

Despite the darkness, I cast an eye over my surroundings for any sign of the returning Silver Fox. It felt late, although I had no idea what *late* actually felt like.

Maybe it was *eleven o'clock late.*

Time to dig up the grave.

'I don't suppose you've seen my fellow gravedigger, have you?' I asked.

Father O'Garble didn't reply. And, by the sound of his snoring, he wasn't about to.

With Fox nowhere to be seen, I decided to get started without him and set off in search of Shiny Diamonds. I moved slowly, my spade out at arm's length for safety reasons. That way, if I happened to stumble upon any more open graves, she would fall in first. Yes, *she*. That's what I said. Brenda and I had spent a lot of time together recently and grown very close. Yes, *Brenda*. It's as good a name as any. Solid and reliable. A lot like the spade itself.

'I think this is it.' I half-expected Brenda to answer as I came to a halt at a dome-shaped headstone that had been clumsily inserted into a roughly covered grave. Crouching down, I pressed my nose up to its surface so I could see what had been engraved on the front.

'*Here lies Shiny Diamonds,*' I read out loud. '*Born ... in the mines. Died ... today. Gone ... for the time being. Rest in peace ... but not forever.*'

That was all the confirmation I needed. Taking a hold of the headstone, I gave it a sharp tug and pulled it out of the earth.

Now it was Brenda's turn to get busy.

The coffin had only been buried that afternoon, but it still took nearly all my strength to dig up the dirt that covered it. I'm not making excuses, but it was so dark I could barely see my own eyeballs. If only I could find a way to illuminate the entire cemetery …

And then, as if by magic, it happened.

Suddenly I could see.

Kind of. If I'm being honest, I couldn't really see at all. Yes, there was light, but the glow was so powerful that I had to turn away and shield my eyes. My ears, however, were free to hear the screech of skidding tyres, followed by the pungent stench of burning rubber. When I dared to look again I was surrounded by cars. Those of the flashing light variety.

'*We are the police.*'

Yes, I had figured that much out for myself. The police cars – five of them in total – dipped their headlights, enabling me to see a little better. Stood in the centre of the vehicles was an ordinary-looking man with a neat haircut, thin moustache and pointed chin. He was dressed in a beige trench coat and black gloves. A megaphone was pressed to his lips, although that only highlighted the fact that every word he spoke arrived with a sharp whistle, almost as if his teeth didn't fit together properly.

'*Do not try to run!*'

'Oh, I don't need to *try*,' I shouted back. 'Running's much like walking, just slightly faster. Although running a bath I'm not so good at. Now, if you don't mind, Brenda and I were just about to dig up this coffin—'

'*You are under arrest!*'

'*Under arrest?*' I repeated. 'Surely you must have me confused with someone else—'

'*There is no confusion. Take him down!*'

I was about to ask where he was going to *take me down* to (preferably somewhere a little warmer with a chocolate fountain) when I was knocked clean off my feet by a single police officer. Unfortunately, it didn't stop there. At last count there were eleven ... no, *twelve* ... no, *thirteen* of them, all on top of me, their helmets, truncheons and padded vests only adding to the pain I was suffering.

We stayed like that for as long as it took the man in the trench coat to wander over to where we lay. From my position at the bottom of the heap, he seemed to be walking at a very slow pace. Almost as if he was doing it on purpose.

'Get him up.' One by one, my fellow *heapsters* leapt to their feet, before the last of them dragged me to mine. 'I'm Detective Inspector Spite of the Special Smuggling Squad,' whistled the man in the trench coat (which couldn't have been easy with all those *S*'s). 'And you are ...?'

'No, I'm not,' I argued. 'You're the only Detective Inspector Spite that I know. I, however, am Pink Weasel. But you can call me Pinky.' Recalling how Duke Majestic had refused my offer of a handshake, I decided upon a different approach altogether and kissed Spite softly on both cheeks. 'Your timing is impeccable by the way,' I continued. 'Let me show you what I was about to do—'

'Oh, I *know* exactly what you were about to do,'

remarked Spite, wiping his face on his sleeve. 'Father O'Garble tipped us off that there was a strange boy prowling around the cemetery and now we've caught you red-handed. Pink Weasel, I'm arresting you on suspicion of smuggling diamonds into Crooked Elbow. You do not have to say anything, but anything you do say will most probably be ignored completely. Right, let's get him cuffed, shall we?'

My head and heart sank simultaneously as one officer took Brenda whilst the other twelve fought over who was going to slap on the handcuffs.

As far as Detective Inspector Spite was concerned, the police had their man.

It was just a shame that the man was a boy.

And the boy was Pink Weasel.

And Pink Weasel is Hugo Dare.

And Hugo Dare is me.

21.'GET IN THE COFFIN!'

Before I could protest, two police officers grabbed me roughly by the dressing gown and dragged me towards the nearest police car.

'*Wait!*' Detective Inspector Spite moved the megaphone away from his lips and waved it in the direction of the grave. 'We're not in any rush,' he said. 'Let's dig up this coffin before we take him back to the station.'

It was only then that I noticed something quite incredible. How I hadn't spotted it when I had kissed him was beyond me, but there it was, as clear as the nose on his face (or just under his nose to be precise).

'You're making a terrible mistake,' I insisted.

'That's what they all say,' smirked Spite.

'*Do they?*' I said, surprised. 'Then why don't you take their advice and grow a real one? Because the one you've painted above your top lip looks more like a stuffed beetle than a moustache.'

'*Why you——!*' Spite stepped forward, placing his full weight on my slippers. He smelled strongly of shoe polish. And I knew why. Not only had he used it to plaster his hair to one side, but he was also wearing a large dollop of it right there in the centre of his face.

'That's a fake moustache ... and if you come any closer I'll prove it!' I said.

Spite backed away. 'Get that coffin out now!' he shouted. 'Let's see what's inside.' He stared at me in disgust as his fellow officers set to work. 'But then you already know what's inside, don't you, Weasel?' he said smugly.

'Of course I do,' I replied. 'Diamonds.'

'Ah! So you admit it!' cried a wide-eyed Spite.

'Why wouldn't I?' I shrugged. 'Knowing that there are diamonds inside a coffin isn't a crime. Especially when I wasn't the one who put them there in the first place.'

'Save your excuses for the judge and jury,' Spite sneered.

I knew it wouldn't get that far. At least, I *hoped* it wouldn't. Surely the Big Cheese would come to my rescue before it reached the courtroom. Nevertheless, I still felt a tightness in my tum as I watched the thirteen officers pull the coffin out of its muddy resting place.

Dropping it down on the grass, they quickly set about unscrewing the lid. I crossed my fingers that they wouldn't be able to get it open. Then I double-crossed them that Silver Fox had been wrong about everything. That there wasn't a huge stash of diamonds in there at all, but a real-life rotting corpse.

Like everything else in the Pearly Gates Cemetery, my hopes died a sad and sorry death the moment the lid to the coffin was pushed to one side.

Fox had been right; it was full of diamonds.

Lots of them.

Hundreds.

Thousands.

Hundreds of thousands.

Far too many to count, even if I took off my slippers and started on my toes.

Spite plunged a hand into the coffin, letting the diamonds run through his fingers. 'Oh, this is most unfortunate ... *for you, Weasel!*'

With a satisfied grin, he stood up and beckoned his officers to gather around. Once they were huddled together, he spoke quietly so I couldn't hear. His words were greeted with a murmur of agreement and the occasional nod of the head. Suddenly the officers split. Twelve of them knelt down around the coffin, whilst the thirteenth hurried over to the nearest police car. Climbing inside, he started the engine and slowly reversed the vehicle. Spite waited for it to stop and then pulled opened the boot. It was empty. Although something told me it wouldn't stay that way for long.

Four minutes later the last diamond had been removed from the coffin and the car's boot was full to its sparkling brim. Job done, the thirteen officers looked towards Spite, who gave them the thumbs up. That was their cue to get into their respective vehicles. I turned away as the headlights flashed in my eyes. When I turned back, they had all driven off.

Almost all.

'And then there were two,' said Spite. With his back resting against the only remaining police car (the one with all the diamonds stored safely inside), he had one eye fixed on the cemetery gates and the other on me. We had only just met, but I didn't trust him (or his shoe polish moustache) in the slightest.

And if that was the case, then maybe it was time we went our separate ways.

'Going somewhere?' asked Spite, as I began to tip-toe backwards into the darkness.

'*Going? Me?* What would I possibly want to do that for?' I said innocently. 'I'm having a lovely time.'

Spite picked up Brenda and pointed her at my face. 'One wrong move from you, Weasel, and I'll be forced to use this spade,' he snarled. '*And it won't be to dig up the ground!* Now, sit down and make yourself comfortable. I've got a call to make.'

I did as he asked, although the comfortable bit wasn't so easy to achieve, especially once the damp grass had soaked through my pyjamas. Spite, oblivious to my woes, pulled a mobile from his trench coat and tapped violently at the screen. I heard it ring several times before it was eventually answered.

'Get Duke,' said Spite sternly. 'Yes, that's right ... *Duke Majestic.*'

There was a slight delay whilst whoever had answered the call went to fetch the leader of the Majestic Mob. During this time, Spite ran a hand over his top lip, carelessly smearing his *moustache* across his cheek as he did so.

'Duke, it's me,' said Spite, his voice echoing around the cemetery. 'That's right ... your favourite policeman. I'm at the Pearly Gates ... yes, your diamonds are safe ... but they're not where you buried them ... no, of course it wasn't me who dug them up ... and, yes, you can have them ... but only for a price. I'm thinking double what you gave me last time.' Spite hesitated. 'There is one slight ... *inconvenience*,' he said, glancing at me. 'It's nothing I can't deal with, though ... just get over here as soon as possible and we'll make the switch ... *no, I just told you*,' added Spite, under his breath. 'By the time you arrive at the Pearly Gates, there won't be an *inconvenience*.'

My nostrils flared with anger as Spite ended the call. 'You're going to hand those diamonds over to the Majestic Mob and they're going to give you money!' I cried.

'That's not strictly true,' said Spite. 'They're not just going to give me money – they're going to give me *lots* of money. Enough to live out the rest of my life in the sunshine.'

'Well, I hope you forget to pack the sun cream,' I scowled. It took me a moment before my brain stepped up a gear. 'So, you knew all along that the diamonds had nothing to do with me.'

'Obviously,' Spite laughed. 'The Majestic Mob are a family of professional criminals involved in the highly lucrative business that is diamond smuggling. You, on the other hand, are nothing but a puny punk in an over-sized dressing gown who just happened to be in the wrong place at the wrong time.' Crouching down, Spite began to push the empty coffin along the grass. 'Bad luck,' he smirked.

'I don't believe in luck,' I said.

'Well maybe you should start,' replied Spite, as the coffin fell back into the open grave. 'Because if you want to see tomorrow then you're going to need it. Now get in.'

'*Get in?*' I climbed up off the grass and looked around. 'Get in ... *what?*'

'Get in the coffin!' ordered Spite.

'*Get in the coffin?*' I held my ground. 'You do know that I'm still alive, don't you?'

'For now,' said Spite. 'The thing is, Weasel, you're the *inconvenience* I was talking about. I promised Duke Majestic that you wouldn't be here by the time he arrived to pick up his diamonds ... and that's a promise I aim to keep. So get in!'

'Oh, do I have to?' I moaned. 'Like, *really* have to. As in *really* really—'

I stopped suddenly as Spite grasped Brenda in both hands like a baseball bat. 'Dead or alive, you're going to end up in that coffin, Weasel, so you might as well save me a job.'

'Well, when you put it like that ...' Stepping forward, I hopped down into the grave. Like it or not, it was my only option. My hands were tied. Or, in this case, handcuffed.

'Lay down,' demanded Spite.

'I'm not tired,' I said.

'No, but I am,' replied Spite, jabbing Brenda towards me. 'I'm tired of you. *Now lay down!*'

'Okay, okay, keep your shoe polish on.' I did as he instructed and laid down in the coffin. It wasn't all that bad really. I mean, not exactly shedroom spacious, but at least I could wriggle my toes.

'I once read that it takes five hours and thirty minutes before all the oxygen in a coffin has been consumed,' began Spite, as he threw Brenda to the ground. 'I guess that's how long you've got left to live. Unless you can escape, of course. Which, let's be serious, Weasel, you can't. Feel free to enjoy your last few hours on Earth though.'

'Don't worry, I will,' I said snottily. 'And, for your information, I'll be under the earth, not on it ... *oh, that's just rude!*

To my dismay, Spite had picked up the lid and slammed it down on the coffin, plunging me into an all-consuming darkness. I tried to push against it, but my hands were still cuffed and my knees weren't strong enough. When I stopped shuffling about, I could hear the screws being returned to their original positions. It was followed by the sound of dirt being shovelled over the coffin.

Spite was right. There was no escape from this. I was trapped underground with five hours and thirty minutes left to live. No, make that five hours, twenty-nine minutes and forty-two seconds. The clock was ticking.

The countdown had begun.

22.'BETTER FELT NEVER.'

Time dragged in the coffin.

With every passing second, my heart beat faster and fear set in that little bit more. Don't get me wrong; it wasn't the lack of oxygen that was causing me such distress. Well, not yet anyway. No, I was more concerned about my rumbling, grumbling belly. I don't know why but I always get hungry when I'm doing absolutely nothing ... and this was as close to *absolutely nothing* as you can possibly get!

I took several deep breaths and tried to swallow them whole, but not even that could satisfy my hunger needs. Then I closed my eyes and tried to think of something other than food. All I had to do was relax. Enjoy the peace and quiet. Marvel at the wonderful sights that surrounded me.

Who was I trying to kid?

I was trapped inside a wooden box.

Buried alive.

Left to rot.

The worms would have a field day when they wriggled upon me. I was like breakfast, lunch and dinner all rolled into one. With enough left over for supper. And then after

THE GREATEST SPY WHO NEVER WAS

that, when the worms had finished filling their faces, there'd be nothing left except a pile of old bones. Oh, and my father's dressing gown, of course.

By now I was panicking so much that I failed to recognise the sound of dirt being shifted from the coffin. Nor did I feel the coffin itself being lifted from out of the grave. And, if I'm being perfectly honest, I was completely unaware that the screws had been removed. In fact, the first I knew about the lid being lifted off was when I opened my eyes and saw that the lid had been lifted off.

Freedom.

Crawling out of the coffin, I took in huge gulps of fresh air as I collapsed face-first on the damp grass. I had done it. I had survived the *un-survivable*. It had been tough, but I was still here. Still alive. *In your face, worms!* For now, at least, they would have to go hungry.

As it turns out, I hadn't needed the full five hours and thirty minutes of oxygen that Spite had promised.

Nevertheless, those one hundred and twenty seconds spent trapped under the ground had been the longest two minutes of my life.

'Thank you,' I panted. Rolling over, I half-expected to see that it was Silver Fox who had come to my rescue.

My expectations, however, were way off.

It was Wrinkles.

With my head in her sights, the old woman raised the spade (*my Brenda!*), took aim and then swung it smoothly like a golf club. Still handcuffed, I had no other option but to sit up straight and hope for the best. My hopes were realised as the spade *swooshed* through the air, missing me by a whisker. The lack of any contact caught Wrinkles momentarily off balance, giving me time to scramble to my feet. Now I was ready for when she came again.

With Brenda at arm's length like a jouster's lance, Wrinkles steadied herself and then lunged towards me. She was about to strike when, without warning, her arm dropped and the spade fell to the ground. Her attention had been drawn to something over my shoulder. I followed her gaze and spotted a police car moving slowly through the cemetery, heading towards the exit.

'If you've come for the diamonds then you're too late,' I said. 'Detective Inspector Spite's got them in the boot of that ... *oh, don't mind me!*'

Like a whippet with a rocket strapped to its back, Wrinkles shoved me to one side before weaving in and out of the graves as she sped through the cemetery grounds. When I tried to follow I was less of a whippet and more like a giraffe on ice, slipping and sliding with every step. Admittedly, any combination that included slippers and wet grass was always going to fail miserably in a sprint-off. Nevertheless, I wasn't about to give up. Not now. Not ever. Nothing could stop me.

Except perhaps the out-stretched legs of Father O'Garble.

He was still fast asleep with his back against the gravestone when I tripped over his ankles and fell flat on my face. I tried to ignore the pain (practically impossible) as I lifted my head (slightly more impossible) and pushed myself up off the grass (nigh on impossible).

'Who's there!' cried O'Garble.

'Not who … Hugo … *oh, forget it!*' I said, cutting myself short.

Back on the move, I had Wrinkles firmly in my sights. To my surprise, she had come to a halt. Something (and it certainly wasn't me) had stopped her in her tracks.

Then I stopped too, barely able to believe what I was seeing.

With its headlights on full beam, the hearse had appeared from out of the shadows and was now racing through the grounds of the cemetery. As far as I could tell it was heading straight for Spite's police car.

And it wasn't about to slow down.

I looked away moments before the inevitable *crunch*. When I turned back the two vehicles were pressed together in a metallic embrace, smoke rising from their bonnets. I moved forward and saw a body slumped over the steering wheel in the hearse, completely motionless. Attached to it was a head. And attached to that was a shock of grey hair resting on the dashboard.

Silver Fox.

My eyes shifted as the door to the police car dropped off and Spite emerged through the opening. Wobbling from side to side, he seemed unsteady on his feet as he made his way around to the boot. So unsteady, in fact, that I guessed it wouldn't be long before he fell over.

And that was what he did.

With a little help from Wrinkles.

Leaping up on top of the police car, she took a running jump and launched herself at the Detective Inspector. I knew from past experience that she was a good shot with her knitting bag and now Spite knew that too. As Wrinkles struck him firmly on the temple, his body went limp and he crashed against the car.

Over and out.

Wrinkles didn't hang around to admire her good work. Opening up the car's boot, she began to scoop huge handfuls of diamonds into her knitting bag. I, meanwhile, had a decision to make. I could either get after her or I could check up on Silver Fox.

Easy-peasy.

Truth was I didn't care one jot about the diamonds.

But I did (curiously) care about Silver Fox.

He was still sprawled over the steering wheel when I reached the hearse. Not for the first time, he was wearing nothing but his underpants. That probably explained why he had failed to meet me at the cemetery. He must've run into Wrinkles on the way and been held up.

With my hands still cuffed, I put my head through the open window and poked my nose into Silver Fox's ear. 'Are you okay?'

'*Better felt never,*' he mumbled. Now I'm no doctor, but Fox didn't appear to be in the best of health. Not only were his eyes popping out of their sockets, but his neck was rolling about on his shoulders as if he had lost control of his muscles. 'Diamonds need I to get after those,' he said bizarrely.

'You need to get after those diamonds,' I said, once I'd translated it. 'You'll be lucky! They've gone!'

'Gone!' Fox groaned. 'Stole them who? *Mob Majestic?*

'No, it was Wrinkles.' I could hear sirens in the distance. 'The police will be here soon,' I said. 'As will the Majestic Mob. Spite called them. He was going to exchange their diamonds for money.'

'Sense makes,' nodded Fox, although he himself was making anything but. 'Going are you where?'

My attempts to wander off unnoticed had failed miserably. 'I don't think I should be here when Duke Majestic arrives,' I explained. 'You'll be alright. He likes you. You're his favourite gravedigger … *wow!* That's colourful!'

I ducked down behind the hearse as the cemetery was lit up by a rainbow of headlights. Both the police and the Majestic Mob had arrived at the Pearly Gates at exactly the same moment.

If ever there was a time for me and my slippers to slip away, it was now.

I gave Silver Fox a little wave and then set off, swerving between the gravestones as, one by one, the vehicles came to a shuddering halt beside me. I passed two more police cars, but neither driver gave me a second glance. Maybe the sight of a young boy racing through the cemetery in an over-sized dressing gown and pyjamas was just too scary a thought to contemplate.

Realising their mistake, the Majestic Mob began to reverse their vehicles in a desperate bid to escape. As luck would have it, the police did much the same thing as they tried to stop them. I didn't wait to see who came out victorious. I was already through the gates when I realised that the fact they were open wasn't a trap at all. Oh well, my mistake. Still, better to be safe than sorry.

Without flipping a coin, I chose right over left and pounded the pavement as fast as my slippers would let me. The streets were deserted. The good (and even the not so good) people of Crooked Elbow knew better than to stray out after dark. It wasn't safe. Anything could happen. And most of *it* already had.

I kept running for as long as possible (six minutes and thirty-seven seconds) until a long day finally took its toll. First, I began to stagger, before the stagger turned to a stumble. I tried in vain to stay on my feet, but my legs crumpled and I collapsed onto the pavement. Ah, that felt better. Hard, yes. Wet, yes. But still better.

I stayed there for well over a minute before forcing myself to look up. Incredibly, I had made it. *It* being Takeaway Way. Number sixty-six to be precise.

The Impossible Pizza.

Also known as the SICK Bucket.

I peered through the window for any sign of Impossible Rita, but the blinds were down and the lights were out. There was no way I could try the secret twist (three times to my left, then twice to my right) with my hands still cuffed, so I chose, instead, to wander over to the door and knock twice with my forehead. *No answer.* I followed that up by lifting the letterbox with my nose and then shouting through it. My shouts, however, turned to screams when my tongue got caught in the slit and I had to pull it out.

I let the tears trickle down my cheeks as I considered my options. I could either stay where I was and wait it out until either the Big Cheese or Impossible Rita decided to return, or I could head for home. If the first option was bad (a bitterly cold night with only a dressing gown for protection), then the second was bad times two with an extra scoop of badness stuck on the side. If I went back to Everyday Avenue now I'd probably never see the light of day again. Just like Bertie and Jasper and the rest of those garden gnomes, I'd be shut away in a room, trapped forever, unless Doreen decided it was safe enough for me to ever leave. Which, let's be serious, she never would.

The bells at Crooked Church chimed midnight as yesterday became today. Saturday was over and Sunday had only just begun. Settling down on the doorstep, I tried to make sense of my first day as a fully-fledged spy. The Big Cheese may have put me with the best – my good buddy Silver Fox – but, in all honesty, things couldn't have gone much worse. Not only had the Bottle Bank been robbed and a coffin's worth of diamonds been stolen from the Pearly Gates Cemetery, but I had been there on both occasions. And on both occasions I had been beaten by a gruesome old grandma who was fleet of foot and nifty with a knitting bag.

Wrinkles was fast becoming my arch enemy. My nemesis. That tiny spot at the back of your nose that makes your eyes water when you try to pick it. For her to be in exactly the right place at exactly the right time not once but twice had to be more than just a coincidence. Someone had to be feeding her information. The kind of information that you could only find deep in the bowels of the SICK Bucket. *Top secret. Highly sensitive. Strictly confidential.* The idea that there was a mole (not the furry variety) within SICK was starting to make more and more sense. And if I could catch the mole, then I was sure it would lead me to Wrinkles.

All of that, however, would have to wait until first light. Then I could meet with the Big Cheese and find out whether my life as a spy had lasted more than twenty-four hours.

For me, first light couldn't come quick enough.

23.'THIS IS YOUR SURPRISE, UGO DAYER.'

First light, predictably, took an absolute age to arrive.

It was my own fault. I had slept so much the previous day at the Pearly Gates Cemetery that I didn't feel tired. Instead, I just sat there, my head resting against the door to The Impossible Pizza, and let my mind wander. The only time my *wanderings* were interrupted was when a loud rumble echoed around Takeaway Way. It seemed to come and go and then come back again. At one point I thought it was an elephant. Then a helicopter. Then an earthquake. Then an elephant escaping from an earthquake in a helicopter.

Then I realised it was me.

Or rather my stomach. And I had no control over that grumbling monster.

I was so hungry that, for one desperate moment, I even considered eating my father's dressing gown. Thankfully, salvation arrived in the form of something so spectacular across the road from where I was sat that I feared my eyes might explode with joy.

It was a café.

The sign above the door read *The Bulging Bellyful.* If nothing else, it sounded like my kind of establishment. Quantity over quality. The more you ate, the sicker you felt. Now all I had to do was wait for it to open.

Exactly twelve minutes and forty-one seconds later, the bells at Crooked Church tolled seven and The Bulging Bellyful came alive. The lights flickered, the blinds shot up and the door swung to one side. Eager for what lay in wait, I clambered to my feet in search of food. Everywhere felt stiff except my stomach. That just felt empty.

I spotted a menu stuck to the window as I made my way across the road. On closer inspection, it wasn't a menu at all. Just one word written in big, bold letters.

GRUB.

They say that dreams don't come true, but whoever said that has clearly never been stood in my slippers. Grub was undoubtedly my favourite type of food, largely because it meant anything and everything. In fact, I was so excited I was already licking my lips in anticipation as I walked inside.

I didn't get far, however, before my dreams fell flat on their face. Just two steps, in fact. Two steps and then my vision was impaired by wave upon wave of billowing black smoke, whilst my nostrils were invaded by the kind of stink that makes bread – both white and brown – run for cover.

It was the smell of burnt toast.

I took another step and accidentally kicked a chair, sending it sliding across the floor.

'Watch where yer goin', ya daft beggar! If ya wants food

you only 'ave to ask!'

The voice howled like a cat in quicksand. I tried to follow it, but hit a dozen more chairs and several tables before I finally collided with what appeared to be the counter. Better late than never, the smoke started to clear. Suddenly I could see ... *and yet just as suddenly I wished I couldn't!*

Lurking behind the counter was something so unnaturally unpleasant that I figured I must still be asleep at the Pearly Gates Cemetery. To be frank, the woman (if that's what *it* was) stood before me was like something out of a horror movie (not that Frank would ever dare say that to her face). I just hoped she couldn't read my mind, although judging by the vacant look on her face she probably couldn't read her own mind, so I wasn't overly concerned.

'The name's Grot,' spat the woman. 'Welcomes to ma Bulging Bellyful.'

I wiped her spittle from my cheeks before it soaked into my skin. I hope you haven't just eaten because I'm about to paint a picture of Grot that will make you reach for the nearest sick bowl. From the top (don't panic, I'm not about to mention her bottom), her hair was purple in colour and fell limply over her eyes, both of which pointed in different directions. Her nose was hooked and home to more warts than your average warthog, whilst her skin was the colour of week-old cat sick. She had too many chins to count and a neck that had been completely swallowed up by shoulders that almost touched the lobes of her crumpled cauliflower ears. At first glance she appeared to be wearing a grubby white apron and little else. There wasn't a second glance. I didn't dare. Just in case *little else* turned out to be *nothing else.*

'This is ma place,' remarked Grot, dribbling all over the counter as she spoke. 'Gristle be the cook and I be the owner, the cleaner and the wait … wait … wait … *wait a minute.*' She stopped talking and stuck a finger up each nostril and a thumb in her ear. She remained silent whilst she rummaged around for a bit, before finally removing all three digits. There was something black and crusty on the tip of each finger and a large lump of wax on her thumb. Satisfied with her *finds*, Grot rolled it all together and then flicked it over my shoulder. '*Ya hungry?*' she asked.

'I *was.*' Fortunately, I'm not easily put off when it comes to food. 'I mean, *I am*,' I said. 'I'm absolutely starving. What do you recommend?'

'What does I recommends?' Grot stopped to think. It was painful to watch. 'I recommends ya go someplace else,' she said honestly.

'I just want something to eat,' I pleaded.

'On yer head be it,' shrugged Grot (and, believe me, it's not easy to shrug when you've got no neck). 'But be warned. I've been closed down eleven times already this year. This is ma twelve re-openin' and ya is ma first customer. If ya pukes yer guts up you'll probably be ma first *and* ma last. It'll be even worse if ya drops down dead!'

'It's a risk I'm prepared to take,' I insisted.

Grot opened her mouth and coughed in my face. Her breath reeked of the sewerage farm in the neighbouring town of Stinking Rump. Maybe she had been there for a holiday.

I know I've always wanted to. 'I supposes,' continued Grot, 'ya could always try ma Breakfast Surprise.'

'It sounds heavenly,' I said. 'What's the surprise?'

'How do I knows?' yelled Grot. 'Gristle has to catch it first ... *then ya can eats it after!*' Grot turned and banged her fist on the wall behind her. 'One Breakfast Surprise, lover boy,' she screeched.

'One Breakfast Surprise comin' up,' hollered a voice from the kitchen. I guessed that *lover boy* was Gristle. If his appearance matched his voice then he was probably an even more hideous version of Grot. That went some way to explaining why she was serving the customers and he was out of sight in the kitchen. As hard as it was to believe, Grot was the *face* of The Bulging Bellyful. And if she was the beauty, I had no wish to meet the beast.

'*Surprise* spotted,' yelled Gristle. 'It's hidin' behind the bins. Gimme a minute and I'll have it in ma fryin' pan.'

Grot smiled at me. She had four teeth practically swinging from her gums, each of them a different shade of black. 'Sits yourself down,' she said, waving me away. 'I'll brings it over.'

I did as she asked in case she spoke again and one of those teeth popped out and hit me where it hurts. Finding a seat amongst so many empty chairs, however, wasn't as easy as it sounds. I needed to sit somewhere I could keep an eye on Grot as well as an eye on The Impossible Pizza. As luck would have it, I've got two eyes. As luck *wouldn't* have it, I've also got the same number of nostrils, which probably explains why I chose the table furthest away from the counter.

'Ya thirsty?'

I had barely sat down when I almost toppled off my chair. For someone with all the grace of a three-legged hippopotamus, Grot had managed, somehow, to creep up on me unnoticed. She was so close I could feel her stubble tickling the back of my neck. Again, I refused to look beyond her apron for fear of what lay underneath. Instead, I concentrated on her hairy hands. They were carrying a large glass vase, which in turn carried a strange lime green concoction that was bubbling away like a toxic trump in a swimming pool.

'I didn't order that,' I said, as the liquid spilled over the rim, running down Grot's six fingers.

'Never said ya did,' Grot argued. 'Gristle made it for ya. He uses leftovers and scrag ends. Whisks it all together with his bare hands. Calls it his Bellyful of Brown.'

'And yet it's green,' I said, just in case neither her nor lover boy had noticed.

'Anyone who drinks it can have a second for free,' continued Grot.

I screwed up my face. '*A second for free?* I wasn't planning on paying for this one.'

'Ya don't haves to,' insisted Grot. 'It's on the house.'

'That's very kind of you,' I lied. I stood up and turned around. 'As you can see, however, my hands are currently—'

Grot didn't wait for me to finish as she grabbed the handcuffs and snapped them off my wrists. 'Now there's nuthin' to stop ya,' she said firmly. 'Drink up.'

Never one to shy away from a freebie, I held my nose

with one hand as I picked up the vase with the other. Placing it to my lips, I took a deep breath. After three.

Three ... two ... one-and-a-half ... one-and-two-ninths ...

Try as I might, I couldn't do it. Grot shook her head in disgust (*or do I mean she shook her disgusting head?*) and then stomped back behind the counter. Left to my own devices, I raised the vase for a second time. I was about to take a sip when I sensed a presence at my shoulder.

'You ordered the Breakfast Surprise?'

I slowly lowered the vase and turned around. There was someone lurking behind me.

Someone far more dangerous than Grot (although nowhere near as revolting).

'This is your surprise, Ugo Dayer.'

I watched as Murder walked around the table. Dressed balaclava-to-toe in black, he seemed to be getting shorter every time I saw him. 'I do hope I is not too much of a disappointment,' he said quietly.

'Just a little,' I said, trying to remain calm. 'Call me ungrateful, but I was hoping the *surprise* would be something I could actually nibble on.'

'Then nibble on this!' said Murder, as he snatched my knife and fork up off the table.

Let battle commence.

I ducked down in my chair as Murder swiped with the knife and then prodded with the fork. He missed with both, but that was just for starters. Soon he would bring the main course. And, judging by his weapons of choice, he wouldn't stop until he had carved me up into tiny, bite-size pieces.

Murder sliced and I swivelled. He stabbed and I swerved. He was getting closer every time.

I, however, only had one chance and I couldn't afford to miss.

As Murder came again, I grabbed the Bellyful of Brown and threw the frothy green liquid at the only part of his body that wasn't hidden.

His eyes.

Murder stopped mid-lunge as tears began to stream down his balaclava. Dropping the knife and fork, he then fell to the floor and began to roll about in agony. Whatever was in that vase, it had exceeded expectations. It was only supposed to obscure his vision, not blind him for life.

'Yer Breakfast Surprise is ready,' bawled Grot, as she bulldozed her way out of the kitchen.

'I'm not really that peckish anymore,' I said, heading towards the exit. 'Although, I'm sure my friend would appreciate it … *if he ever stops crying!*'

I burst out of The Bulging Bellyful and stormed across the road before Grot could protest. I was all set to try the door to The Impossible Pizza when I felt a tug on my dressing gown. I spun around, half-expecting to see Murder behind me, armed with something more threatening than a knife and fork.

I was wrong.

'Fancy seeing you here,' I panted. 'I didn't think postmen worked on a Sunday.'

'*They don't.*' The postman removed an envelope from his bundle and waved it in front of my face. 'I've got a letter for you, Master Hugo Dare, also known as Pink Weasel.'

'Pinky to my friends,' I said. I took the letter and settled down on the doorstep.

Pink Weasel,
The doorstep of The Impossible Pizza,
Takeaway Way,
Crooked Elbow.

I looked up, confused. 'How do you always know where I'm going to be?'

'I don't,' admitted the postman. 'But the Big Cheese does. He knows everything. He even knows things that will probably never happen.'

I ripped the envelope apart with my teeth and a slip of paper fell onto my lap. The message, as always, was short and to the point.

Where are you?
I'm waiting in the Pantry.
The Big Cheese.
P.S Did I tell you I was waiting?
P.P.S Because I am. Waiting, I mean. So hurry up!

I read it several times before the postman cleared his throat. 'You do realise that in five seconds time that message will—'

'I know, I know,' I said, interrupting him. 'The message will ... *ouch!*

I jumped up in horror as the slip of paper burst into flames whilst resting in my lap. Fearful for my father's dressing gown, I tossed it into the air before it shrivelled up into nothing.

'You'd better go in,' said the postman, nodding towards The Impossible Pizza.

He was right. Without the handcuffs, I finally managed to twist the doorknob. Three times to my left, then twice to my right. Unlike last night, the door opened.

When I looked again, the postman had gone.

And, moments later, so too, had I.

24. 'THE LIFE OF A SPY IS ANYTHING BUT PREDICTABLE.'

'D'yer wanna' pizza me?'

I chose to ignore Impossible Rita as I marched into The Impossible Pizza. Reaching under the counter, I pressed the button and then held on to my dressing gown as the building shook and the wall parted to reveal the rubbish chute.

'Hey, that's not fair, Hugo Dare!' cried Rita, wagging an angry finger in my direction. 'I didn't get to say hello.'

'Oh, be my guest.' I stepped back and held out my arms. 'I'm ready when you are.'

Giddy with excitement, Rita clambered up onto the counter and threw herself into the air. Unfortunately for her, she didn't stop to look before she leapt. Unfortunate because that was the exact moment I decided to shuffle ever so slightly to one side.

'That was a stupid thing to do,' groaned Rita, as she peeled her face up off the floor.

'So why did you do it?' I replied smartly. I was still chuckling to myself as I climbed into the chute and let go.

Before I knew it, I was hurtling downwards at a terrifying speed. As expected, Rumble met me with open arms and a bouncy belly and then silently set to work. I was clean. Or rather my pockets were. I myself was caked head-to-toe in mud from my time at the Pearly Gates Cemetery. Thankfully, my favourite ex-wrestler didn't seem to view this as a threat to security.

Cuddling complete, I strode freely across the SICK Bucket, my eyes, as usual, glued to the vision of loveliness that was Miss Felicity Finefellow. To my surprise, she was doing something that almost resembled work. Well, she was writing. That was good enough for me. And probably as good as it ever got.

'*Love letter?*' I asked, bending backwards over her desk for a closer look.

Finefellow snatched at the piece of paper, inadvertently turning it towards me as she did so. I even got to read the top line before she slipped it into her drawer.

Dear the Big Cheese ...

'It's rude to creep up on people,' Finefellow scowled. 'Especially with a face like yours.'

'That's understandable,' I said. 'My beauty can be quite frightening.'

'No, what's frightening is that you're still alive,' said Finefellow. 'I thought we'd finally seen the back of you after what happened at the Pearly Gates.'

'You don't just get to see the back of Hugo Dare,' I said smoothly. 'Not until you've seen the front of him ... I mean ... *me*. Not to mention everything in between.

152

Including the rash I've got just below my—'

'*Enough!*' said Finefellow. 'I'd rather not see *any* of you if I'm being honest.'

'Now we both know *that's* not true.' I leant in for a whiff of Finefellow's perfume, but ended up with a high heel wedged firmly up my left nostril. 'Maybe we could meet up later,' I said, once I'd carefully removed the shoe and placed it back on her foot. 'I know a delightful little restaurant not far from here. *The Bulging Bellyful.* Maybe we could grab a bite to eat.'

'*A bite to eat?*' said Finefellow. 'I'd rather eat my own fingers than spend an evening with you.'

I took a moment to consider her answer. 'So … *is that a yes or a no?*'

'What do you think?' replied Finefellow.

'What do I think?' I pondered. 'You want me to decide? Well, in that case, it's a yes. A *definite* yes. Make a note of it in your diary, Finefellow. *A date with Dare …*'

I hurried away before the Big Cheese's secretary could say something that might change my mind. Women can be awkward like that sometimes.

When I entered the Pantry, the Big Cheese was sat at his writing table looking grumpy. Unlike yesterday, however, there were no half-eaten pizzas keeping him company.

'Not hungry, sir?' I said, lowering my bum into the stiff plastic chair directly opposite him.

'Yes *and* no,' sighed the Big Cheese. 'I'm absolutely famished, but I'm also far too nervous to eat. SICK is in a perilous state, young Dare.'

'It's on its SICK bed, sir,' I joked.

'We're the laughing stock of the spying society,' continued the Big Cheese. 'Talking of which, I heard about what happened at the Pearly Gates Cemetery.'

'Thank you, sir,' I said.

'I wasn't congratulating you,' barked the Big Cheese. 'From what I understand the entire operation was more a failure than a success.'

'If anything it was a combination of the two,' I argued. 'A *failess* perhaps. Or even a *succlure.*'

'I'd call it a downright disaster!' cried the Big Cheese.

'Then I'd call you one teabag short of a cuppa',' I replied. 'Don't forget, sir, Agent One and I did manage to uncover a diamond smuggling ring involving the Majestic Mob and Detective Inspector Spite.'

'And don't *you* forget that you also allowed a coffin-full of diamonds to slip carelessly through your fingers,' added the Big Cheese.

'Unforeseen circumstances, sir,' I explained. 'Wrinkles showed up and—'

'*Wrinkles sprinkles!* roared the Big Cheese. 'You know I don't want to hear that name in my Pantry!'

'But that doesn't mean she doesn't exist,' I said. 'Like it or not, sir, Wrinkles is always one step ahead of me.'

The Big Cheese slammed his hand down on the table. 'Whoever she is, whatever she may be doing, there is no way whatsoever that she has access to top secret SICK intelligence!' he boomed. 'Really, young Dare, this Wrinkles woman is the only thing you ever talk about. Don't you want to know what happened to Agent One?'

'Should I?' I shrugged. 'I mean, of course I do … a little … no, a lot. After all, the last time I saw him he had just crashed a hearse into a police car in nothing but his underpants.'

'The life of a spy is anything but predictable,' nodded the Big Cheese. 'Thankfully, Silver Fox managed to escape from the Pearly Gates and get back to the SICK Bucket in one piece. A few hours' sleep and he's already back out in the field, deep undercover. He's tracking Coocamba's Idol, a rare and priceless artefact, as it … *what's the matter now, young Dare?*'

'Did you just say cucumber, sir?' I said. 'Because that's what my stomach heard and now it's rumbling so loudly I can barely hear myself blink.'

'*Coocamba* – not cucumber!' snapped the Big Cheese. 'Coocamba's Idol is a six-inch wooden statue celebrating the first king of the Coocamba Isles. Not that they really need a king. The entire island is slightly smaller than a football pitch and numbers no more than twenty-three people at any given time. As for the Idol, it arrived in Crooked Elbow by boat last night and it will leave the same way before today has even passed.'

'So where is it now?' I asked.

'Ah, that's where things get a little complicated,' the Big Cheese admitted. 'The Idol's currently being held at Crooked Comprehensive.'

'My school?' I spluttered.

'Regrettably so,' nodded the Big Cheese. 'Delegates from the Coocamba Isles – all one of them – decided that the school would be the ideal place to exhibit the Idol while it's in town. It's so precious that only the great and good of Crooked Elbow will be allowed to view it.'

'Which I'm assuming includes you, sir,' I said.

'Then you assume wrong,' the Big Cheese frowned. 'I'm ... *erm* ... far too busy for such tomfoolery.'

'Of course you are, sir,' I said, winking at the Chief of SICK. 'So, if you're not going, who is?'

The Big Cheese snorted loudly. 'The usual suspects,' he said begrudgingly. 'The Mayor ... several councillors ... one or two other business leaders. Your Headteacher, Miss Stickler, and the librarian, Mrs Trot, are organising things. And let's not forget about the school caretaker.'

'You mean Blind Man Bluff?' I asked incredulously.

The Big Cheese shook his moustache. 'Mr Bluff is on sick leave. He hurt his leg trying to clean his ears.'

'*Wow!* That's unlucky,' I said.

'Not for us it's not,' argued the Big Cheese. 'It left a vacancy that our very own Silver Fox has now conveniently filled. He's there to add security in case someone tries to steal the Idol. That's where you come in, young Dare. You're the new caretaker's even newer assistant.'

'Caretaker's assistant?' I said, screwing up my face. 'Aren't you forgetting something, sir? Miss Stickler and I don't really see eye to eye.'

'Don't worry about Stickler,' the Big Cheese insisted. 'You just keep a low profile, stay close to Agent One and protect the Idol. I'm relying on you, young Dare. Like a dog relies on its fleas.'

'Pleased to hear it, sir,' I said, climbing to my feet. 'And, in case you're wondering, I'm one flea you won't need to get rid of.'

I gave the Big Cheese another curtsy (note to self – please stop curtsying) and then exited the Pantry one small step later. I marched straight past Miss Finefellow without a second glance. Not that she'd have noticed me anyway. Her head was stuck too far under her desk for that. Maybe she was shy. Or just hiding. Either way, she couldn't ignore me forever. At some point she would have to take me seriously, especially once I'd put a stop to Wrinkles and her wrinkly wrongdoings. That sour old stuffing ball was on borrowed time and when I finally caught her I'd be the saviour of SICK. The King of Crooked Elbow. The fine fellow for Miss Felicity Finefellow.

It's funny because the Big Cheese's secretary wasn't the only person who'd be affected by today's developments. Doreen, my mother, would be leaping for joy when she found out the news. Miraculously, her wish had come true.

Her son was going to school at the weekend.

And there was nothing I could do about it.

25.'IT'S ME!'

Crooked Comp' had changed.

Yes, it was still grey and dreary. Yes, it still smelled like a combination of boiled socks and sweaty cabbage. And, yes, the thought of my Headteacher, Miss Stickler, still sent a shiver shooting up my ankles. But the last time I had been here things had been very different. Then the whole place had been a hive of noise and confusion. Chaos lurked at every corner. Chaos *and* water bombs.

That was two days ago.

Today was a Sunday and none of the above were anywhere to be seen.

A lot like students, in fact.

Considering they were normally rubbing shoulders like sardines in a school-shaped tin, it felt strange not to see a single boy or girl from the moment I first set foot on the premises. Unlike me, they were all enjoying their weekend, doing exactly what they wanted.

Which reminded me, I *wanted to* eat so long ago that my belly was now grumbling like a beaver with a bad case of toothache. If I didn't fill it soon it would most probably bid me farewell and find somebody else to hang out with. Somebody who did bother to eat from time to time.

Fortunately for the pair of us, I had a plan.

Striding through the double doors that led into the main body of the school, I made my way towards the only place that even came close to satisfying my hunger needs.

The canteen.

Okay, so it didn't exactly serve food, but it did serve something that *almost* passed for food if you dimmed the lights, turned off your taste buds and let it slide down your throat.

The canteen, like the school itself, was closed so I carried on into the kitchen until I found the fridge. I crossed my fingers and tried to yank it open, but it wouldn't budge. Never one to give up, I uncrossed my fingers and tried again. This time the door swung to one side.

I wasn't expecting much, but what greeted me was even less than that. The fridge was completely bare. No, that's not true. The bottom shelf was actually so full it was practically overflowing. That was the good news. The bad news is that it was overflowing with bones.

I didn't bother to ask myself why they were there, or even if they were human or animal. Instead, I rummaged through them until I found the one that looked the most appetising. Placing it under my nose, I gave it a good sniff.

Then I licked it.

Then I tried to bite it.

My teeth were still vibrating as I put the bone back in the fridge and exited the kitchen. Yes, I was hungry – just not *bone* hungry. Whether my belly liked it or not, the search for food would have to wait.

Out in the corridor, I was back on track and heading (hopefully) for the Boiler Room. That was where the caretaker, Blind Man Bluff, spent most of his time so it made sense to assume that Silver Fox would be there too. Every classroom I passed along the way had its blinds pulled down and its door locked. Occasionally, I pressed my ear to the keyhole, but heard nothing from inside.

Seven steps later I turned a corner and heard a voice at the other end of the corridor. It was instantly recognisable. Like an early morning alarm clock at full volume.

I tip-toed into the shadows, careful not to reveal myself. That was when I saw her.

The Headteacher of Crooked Comp'.

Miss Stickler.

Some things in life make you want to stick your head in a bucket and she was one of those things. As wide as she was tall, her body resembled a watermelon perched precariously on top of a tiny pair of walnut legs. She wore a monocle in her left eye and a white-headed pimple on her right cheek. Her hair, fiery red in colour, was scraped back from her forehead, whilst her tight-fitting, bulge-hugging suit was dark, a lot like her mood.

I looked to Stickler's left and spotted a small boy floating in mid-air. I blinked twice and realised it wasn't a boy at all, but a man.

Mr Peabody.

A teacher (of sorts), he was shorter than most students

and wetter than a lettuce in a bird bath.

'You know the rules,' hissed Stickler. Her fingers were clenched tightly around Peabody's tie as she dangled him above the ground (at least that explained the *floating*). 'Today is a special day. No one is permitted to wander these corridors except me. And you are not me. I am *me!*'

'Yes, you are … no, I'm not … it's just … I was desperate,' pleaded Peabody.

'I don't care that you were desperate,' said Stickler sternly.

'Desperate for the lavatory,' Peabody explained.

'I don't care that you were desperate for the lavatory,' repeated Stickler.

Peabody let out a high-pitched squeal. 'I'm not desperate anymore,' he whimpered soon after.

'I don't care that you're not—' Miss Stickler stopped mid-sentence and peered down at the puddle that had formed under Peabody's hovering feet. Without warning, she let go of his tie and he landed with a *splash*. 'Problem solved,' Stickler smirked. 'Now clean up this mess and then get out of my sight. *And don't you dare stop off at lost property to change your trousers!*'

Peabody knelt down and began to dab at the floor with a handkerchief. When he had finished, he stood up and made his way towards me, his shoes squelching with every step. I pressed my back against the wall as he walked straight past; oblivious to my presence. Once he had gone, I peeked back along the corridor. Before I could come out of the shadows I had to be sure that Miss Stickler had followed her own advice and headed back to the classroom.

As luck would have it, she was already on the move.

As luck *wouldn't* have it, she was *moving* in my direction.

'*Intruder alert! Intruder alert!*' cried Stickler, as she stormed along the corridor. 'Come out with your hands up!'

I ducked out of sight, but it was too late. I had been spotted. Which left me with two options. *Run or hide?* There was always a third option, of course – to do as she asked – but only a complete muffin-head would consider doing that.

Yes, we all know where this is going ...

'Morning, Sticky,' I said, stepping out into the open. '*It's me!*'

'*You!*' Miss Stickler stopped suddenly. 'It can't be ...'

'It can and it is,' I said.

'*Not ... Hugo Dare?*' spluttered Stickler.

'The one and only,' I said.

Miss Stickler violently shook her head. 'Not *the* Hugo Dare?'

'The same one and only,' I insisted.

'*The ... Hugo ... Dare!*' It was more than just Miss Stickler's head that was shaking now – it was her entire body. 'The Hugo Dare who brought a skunk into class and tried to pretend it was a new student,' she hollered. 'The Hugo Dare who locked himself in the stationery cupboard for two weeks solid and ate nothing but pencils. The Hugo Dare who blocked up the entire toilet system with an enormous—'

'*Sshhh!* You're making me blush,' I said. 'Be honest, though, Sticky. Have you missed me these past few days?'

'*Missed you?*' Miss Stickler squeezed her hands together

until her knuckles turned white. 'Oh, I've missed you alright. *I've missed you this much!*'

That was the cue for my Headteacher to charge at me with both fists flailing and feet flapping. It was a frightening combination. So frightening, in fact, that I turned to run. I quickly changed my mind, though, when I looked along the corridor.

There was something there.

Something big and hairy with thick fur, powerful legs and jet-black eyes that silently screamed *I would like to eat you.*

I backed away as it showed its teeth and began to snarl.

A moment later I remembered who I was supposed to be running from when Miss Stickler lifted me up by the scruff of my dressing gown and slammed me against the wall. Like Peabody, I was powerless to fight back. Unlike Peabody, however, I had no intention of wetting myself (not yet, anyway).

'I thought Crooked Comp' had a No Pets policy,' I said.

'Feast is not a pet!' Using her free hand, Miss Stickler clicked her fingers and the beast stopped snarling. 'He's a highly-trained beast from the East of Elbow. Trained to *kill*, of course. Or, at the very least, to seriously injure.'

'Pleased to hear it,' I muttered. If nothing else, it explained all the bones in the fridge. 'Guard dogs in a school, though? Little bit over the top, don't you think?'

'Not when revolting rat droppings like you are wandering about unsupervised!' spat Stickler. 'You're more than just a nuisance, Dare ... *you're nuclear!* You're not just irritating … *you're incendiary*! Trouble I can deal with, but you … *you're like a headache that won't go away!*

'You could always try chopping your head off,' I suggested. 'And, yes, I am willing to provide the axe.'

Stickler's nostrils flared. 'You're nothing but an insufferable little imp. I was hoping you might have seen the error of your ways over the weekend, but you've not changed one bit.'

'Ah, that's where you're wrong,' I said smugly. 'I've changed quite a lot as it happens. And I don't just mean my underpants. Believe it or not, but I'm the caretaker's new assistant.'

Stickler loosened her grip on my dressing gown. 'I am expecting a new assistant, but his name is Mr—'

'Weasel,' I said. 'Yes, that's me.'

'That's not possible,' frowned Stickler. 'You were Hugo Dare on Friday. You can't just change your name.'

'*Can't I?*' I said. 'Really, Sticky, anyone would think I'm an undercover spy the way you keep on interrogating me.'

Whoops.

'That's a curious thing to say,' whispered Stickler, her cold lips brushing against my ear. 'Do you know something you shouldn't?'

'Oh, I know lots of things I shouldn't,' I replied. 'And very few things I should. Not to mention several things in between.'

Unfortunately for me, Miss Stickler wasn't easily confused. 'I don't think you're as stupid as you make out,' she said slowly. 'Are you aware of what we have here at Crooked Comprehensive?'

'I'm certainly not aware of any rotten old carving you might have on display,' I said without thinking.

Double whoops.

'So, you know about Coocamba's Idol then?' said Stickler.

'I've no idea what you're talking about,' I said innocently. 'And even less idea what *I'm* talking about. I'm just a humble caretaker's assistant.'

'So you keep on saying.' Miss Stickler finally released her grip and I slid down the wall. 'If that's the case then get to work before I change my mind,' she cried. 'And, whatever you do, stay away from the library!'

'As you wish,' I said, picking myself up off the floor. 'I'll love you and leave you then, shall I? Well, I'll *leave you* anyway. Oh, one last question. Just a simple thing. Can you tell me where the Boiler Room is, please?'

'No,' replied Stickler, as she turned to leave. 'Find it yourself. Or, better still, don't find it at all!'

With that, Miss Stickler clicked her fingers and Feast the beast took off after her. At that very moment nothing would have a given me greater pleasure than to hurl a slipper at the back of her head, but it was too great a risk. Whether I liked it or not, I wasn't here to gain revenge on my horrendous Headteacher.

I was here to find Silver Fox.

To do that, however, I was first going to have to find the Boiler Room.

And something told me that that was about to happen on the very next page.

26.'DO I LOOK LIKE THE ENEMY?'

I found the door to the Boiler Room almost immediately.

Well, that's if you call wandering along endless corridors for over an hour almost immediately (which, oddly enough, I do). When I finally stumbled upon it (an hour is, admittedly, a particularly long stumble), I was amazed that I had failed to find it earlier. Especially when you consider that *BOILER ROOM* had been printed in big white letters on the front of a bright blue door. Turns out I had walked past it three times already that day. Which goes a long way to explaining why the school seemed much larger than usual and I felt dizzier than a moose on a merry-go-round.

Oh well, fourth time lucky and all that ...

I knocked twice, my eyes darting from left to right as I waited for an answer. Ten ... eleven ... twelve seconds passed. I actually opened the door much earlier than that, but I don't want you to think I'm impatient. I was about to step inside when a random thought bombarded my brain.

Secrets of a Spy Number 42 – never walk knowingly into the unknown.

Now, if I took my own advice I would've shut the door and

waited outside. What I didn't bargain on, however, was another *SoaS*. A rival that made my decision all the more difficult.

Secrets of a Spy Number 61 – bad things come to those who wait.

Ah, problem. Fortunately, the decision was taken out of my hands when I heard a growl at the other end of the corridor. I had company. *Big, hairy* company. And according to Stickler, it was trained to kill.

With no time to waste, I slipped inside the Boiler Room and closed the door before Feast the beast could feast upon me. I was instantly plunged into the kind of darkness that made me wish I'd grown up on a diet of carrots, carrots and more carrots (as opposed to my own diet of liver, gherkins and the occasional bowl of bird seed).

Not to worry. I knew just the trick to cure my momentary blindness.

Secrets of a Spy Number 59 – if you can't see, try looking.

Trust me, it works (especially when you open your eyes).

As far as I could I tell I was surrounded by nothing but bare brick. It was to my left. To my right. Above my head. And even beneath my feet. Or so I thought. Striding forward, I soon realised that this wasn't the case and took a tumble. Eight steps later and I came to a painful halt.

It wasn't the most dignified of entrances but I had arrived in the Boiler Room.

The first thing that struck me was how incredibly hot it was down there. I had a sudden urge to strip off, but decided against it. Only Silver Fox was allowed to do that. And even that wasn't through choice.

The second thing was that I could see. There was a bulb above my head that single-handedly lit up a large cylindrical tank that practically filled the entire room from floor to ceiling. Now I'm not one for making assumptions, but I figured that this was the boiler. I listened as it whirred and hummed, alongside an occasional *creak* and an even less occasional *bang*.

Then I heard something else entirely. A curious moaning, groaning sound. It wasn't coming from the boiler itself, but somewhere behind it. It reminded me of those moments in horror films when a monster rises up from a muddy bog, covered head-to-toe in slime, ready to devour those who have strayed too close.

Luckily, I don't believe in swamp monsters.

Mutant zombies, however ...

With my imagination running wild, I tried to stand, but, somehow, failed tragically. Now, I'm not one for making assumptions, but it appeared as if my legs had been swiped out from under me. Sure enough, the moment I rolled onto my back something long and thin rested on my forehead, pinning me to the ground.

It was a crutch.

Now I'm not one for making assumptions (although that is three in quick succession so perhaps I am), but I guessed that this was what had tripped me up in the first place.

'*Well, bust my banjo! The last thing I expected to find creeping about down here was the enemy!*'

Both the croaky voice and the crutch belonged to a man. He was stood over me, but I couldn't quite make out his face.

'Do I look like the enemy?' I asked, frustrated.

'Indeed you do,' insisted Croaky. 'The enemy comes in all shapes and sizes. Tall or short. Fat or thin. Smartly dressed or wearing rags. Some are even hideously ugly like you.'

'I'll have you know that I'm extremely handsome,' I argued. 'I'm also one of the good guys. My name is Mr Weasel. I'm here to assist the caretaker.'

'*Assist the caretaker?*' Croaky began to chuckle. 'Why would any self-respecting caretaker want to be assisted by a weedy little snotgoblin like you?'

'*That's it!*' With the crutch seemingly glued to my forehead, I sat up and tried to pull it away with both hands. It refused to move, but at least I now knew who I was dealing with.

It was Mr Bluff, the caretaker.

Or, as he was more commonly known at Crooked Comp', Blind Man Bluff.

As appearances go, I wasn't entirely sure which *look* Bluff was going for, but if I had to guess I would probably say it was the *get ready for work whilst still asleep* look. His hair was stuck on end as if it had never been combed, toothpaste was smeared across his forehead and his ears supported not one but two pairs of swimming goggles. From the feet up, he was wearing open-toed sandals with different coloured socks, grey trousers that were far too short in the leg and a coat that can only be described as the type worn by caretakers. Long in length and the colour of sawdust, its pockets were home to all manner of things from paint brushes to hammers, screwdrivers to mousetraps (the latter of which explaining why he reeked so strongly of mouldy cheese).

And then we arrive at Bluff's chin. It upsets me to say it, but it was fully dressed. Dressed in hair. I think you know what I'm talking about, but if you don't, well, prepare yourself because this is about to get very unpleasant.

Blind Man Bluff had a beard.

Any reader with a memory unlike a goldfish will no doubt recall that a man with a beard is not to be trusted (*SoaS Number 22*). The rest of you please pay attention. I don't like beards and beards don't like me. It's that simple. Now, whether he planned it or not, Bluff's beard was everything a beard shouldn't be. Big and bushy with a random assortment of biscuit crumbs and tiny insects hidden inside, it gave me the creeps just looking at it.

'Any chance you could remove your crutch before it makes a hole in my skull?' I said.

'I'll remove mine once you've removed yours, Weasel,' replied Bluff stubbornly.

'*I haven't got a crutch!*' I shouted.

'Well, why didn't you say so?' Blind Man Bluff lowered his arm and the crutch fell away from my face. It was only then that I noticed his left leg. From ankle to thigh, it was bound in a huge plaster cast. Unless it was some kind of bizarre fashion craze that had only caught on amongst caretakers, the cast explained the crutch.

'I heard you'd had an accident,' I said, pushing myself up off the floor. 'That's why I thought there was another caretaker working here. A Mr Fox.'

'I'm the only caretaker at Crooked Comp',' said Bluff proudly. 'Always have been, always will be. Yes, I've been off for a few days, but I'm back now.' He stopped talking and rearranged both pairs of swimming goggles so he could study me more closely. 'You don't look like much, Weasel – probably less than that if I'm being honest – but if you've really come here to assist the caretaker then I suppose you'll have to do. There's a whole heap of jobs waiting for us. Stand up and we'll make a start.'

'I am stood up,' I insisted.

'That's a shame,' said Bluff. 'It's never nice to be stood up by someone.'

'Nobody stood me up,' I said. 'I stood myself up.'

'I didn't know that was possible,' muttered Bluff. He poked me with his crutch and then gestured towards the steps. I wondered if the *poking* was a one-off until he did it again. And again. And again. And …

I was halfway up the steps when the same moaning, groaning sound I had heard earlier started up again. Like before, it seemed to be coming from behind the boiler.

'Can you hear that?' I asked.

Bluff was one step behind me. 'Of course I can,' he replied.

'Do you know what it is?' I said.

'What *what* is?' said Bluff, confused.

'*That sound?*' I said.

'What sound?' shrugged Bluff.

'I thought you could hear it?' I said.

'Hear what?' frowned Bluff.

'Oh, forget it.' The curious moaning and groaning would have to wait. As would Silver Fox. Wherever he was, he wasn't in the Boiler Room. With any luck, I would find him as I went about my chores.

'You'll need one of these,' said Bluff. He handed me a small bundle as we reached the top step. It was a caretaker's coat, just like the one that Bluff himself was wearing. I put it on over my dressing gown, amazed at how well it fitted.

Now I was ready.

Ready to start work as a caretaker's assistant.

27. 'PUT IT BACK WHERE YOU FOUND IT!'

Blind Man Bluff hadn't been joking when he said there was a whole heap of jobs waiting for us.

No, scratch that. *We* didn't have a whole heap of jobs waiting for us at all.

I did.

Whilst Bluff hobbled behind on his crutches, hurrying me along as he croaked out orders, I set to work. I painted walls, cleaned floors, arranged seating, dusted the ceiling, changed light bulbs and marked out an entire football pitch, all in the space of one morning. Admittedly, I did most of it incredibly badly, not that Bluff seemed to care.

'That was tough,' he said, breathing heavily as he leant on his crutch. 'Don't know how I do it sometimes.'

'*You* didn't,' I muttered. I was dead on my feet, which went a long way to explaining why I found myself flat on my back in the middle of the football pitch.

'Still, nothing that a spot of grub can't fix,' said Bluff. Reaching inside his caretaker's coat, he removed a large rectangular lunchbox. 'You did bring some, didn't you?'

'I didn't know I had to,' I said sadly.

'Normally you wouldn't,' admitted Bluff, 'but today's a Sunday. Everything is closed, including the canteen, although I have seen a few teachers wandering about the place. I think it's got something to do with a really old cucumber.'

'Coocamba's Idol,' I said. My nostrils twitched as Bluff opened the lunch box and removed a stack of finely cut sandwiches. 'They smell delicious. Let me guess ... *pickle and banana?*'

'Wrong,' said Bluff, as he munched away. 'They're actually banana and pickle. You can have one if you—'

'*Like*,' I blurted out. 'Yes, I do, thank you very much. I *really* like.'

I tried to stop myself from shaking as Bluff passed me not one but five sandwiches. As every good spy knows, you can't let yourself be distracted by something as simple as several slices of bread and an exotic selection of fillings.

Then I took a bite.

And suddenly Blind Man Bluff was my best friend in the whole of Crooked Elbow.

'That cucumber they've been raving about is in the library,' said Bluff, as we greedily filled our faces. 'It was a little pea that told me that. *A little Peabody.* He reckons the cucumber is priceless. That's why Stickler has told all the teachers to stay at home except a select few. And definitely no kids!'

'*Almost* no kids,' I said, pointing at myself.

'You're different,' argued Bluff. 'You're my assistant. And the enemy.'

'Of course I am.' By now I had decided it was easier to agree with him. 'Where are you going?'

To my obvious dismay, Blind Man Bluff was already on the move. And he was taking his lunch box with him. 'Back to the Boiler Room,' he said. 'We can't sit around all day, Weasel. We've got a lot of work to be getting on with this afternoon.'

'Yes, I'm sure *I* have!' I sighed. I waited until the caretaker was out of sight before I leapt to my feet. There was somewhere I had to be ... *and it wasn't the Boiler Room.*

Blind Man Bluff had let slip that Coocamba's Idol was being displayed in the library so it made perfect sense for me to check it out for myself. Not only that, but Miss Stickler had warned me to stay away, which made it the obvious destination for someone as incredibly awkward as yours truly.

When I got there I avoided the front entrance and headed straight for the back of the building. Satisfied that I couldn't be seen, I slowed my pace and, like an over-cautious crab at high tide, began to work my way along the wall. I stopped when I reached the first window and peeked inside.

How disappointing!

Okay, so maybe balloons and banners, party hats and flashing lights, was a little over the top, but what I hadn't been expecting was the library in all its boring glory. Dull, out-dated and disturbingly drab, it had a lot in common with the librarian herself, an unnaturally horse-like woman called Mrs Trot. Both long in the face and even longer in the tooth, Trot had an unnerving knack of always looking down on anyone who dared to set foot inside her beloved library. If pushed, I'd have to say the best thing about her was her cardigan. Navy blue in colour, it had patches on the elbows and a hole in one armpit. The worst thing about her was *everything else* about her.

I searched for Trot and found her leant over her counter, her beady eyes trained on something or someone that I couldn't quite make out. I swivelled my neck for a better view, but it was no use. My angle was all wrong. What I needed was a change of position.

And I knew just where to find one.

The library, like most buildings I had come across in my young life, had a roof. And on that roof there was a skylight. Now I just had to get up there.

I moved away from the window and headed back the way I had come. That was where I found what I was looking for. No, not a ladder, but the next best thing.

A drainpipe.

Wrapping my legs around the plastic casing, I started to shimmy upwards as quickly as my shimmying skills would allow. The drainpipe wasn't as strong as I presumed and *creaked* under my weight. Then it began to *bend*. With a *crack* and a *snap* sure to follow, I hurried to the top and scrambled over the gutter onto the flat roof. I stared at my hands, shocked to find that they were covered in some kind of white residue. I was about to lick it off when I realised what it was.

Pigeon poop.

It was everywhere I looked, as well as all the places that

my eyes couldn't quite stretch to. In the end I gave in to the inevitable and crawled right through it. When I reached the skylight it was hardly a surprise to find that it, too, was covered in bottom deposits from our feathery friends. I wiped most of it away with the sleeve of my father's dressing gown and looked down into the library. I could see Trot's counter, but the woman herself was no longer behind it.

Then I spotted her. She was directly beneath me, stood beside a plastic plinth that was almost as tall as she was. My first thought was that Trot was going bald on top. My second was that she was looking straight into the eyes of a six-inch wooden statue that was resting on the plinth.

I had found Coocamba's Idol … *and it hadn't been stolen. Yet.*

Turning away from the plinth, Trot galloped back behind her counter before eventually exiting the library. *Out of sight and out of mind.* Just how I liked her.

I had a strong feeling that Wrinkles could strike at any moment and, if she did, what good would I be stranded on the roof, covered in bird droppings. No, a better view of the library was no longer enough for me. What I needed now was a closer look at the Idol.

I had an idea, but it was so stupidly dangerous that only someone dangerously stupid would be able to pull it off.

Digging my nails under the rim of the skylight, I pulled until it eventually flew to one side. What I was about to do next was very risky, but I did it nevertheless. First, I carefully lowered my legs through the opening, before following them not so carefully with the rest of my body. Suddenly I was just hanging there, in the library, by the tips of my fingers. I glanced down and tried not to panic. It was about a six-foot drop to the ground below. Or seven. Or even eight. If I'm being honest, I don't really know how large a foot is so I couldn't tell.

I let go before I could talk myself out of it.

All that mattered what that I didn't hit Coocamba's Idol on my way down.

And I didn't.

But I did hit the plinth.

I struck it with my knee. Not hard enough to knock it over, but enough to make it wobble. Which, in turn, made the Idol wobble.

Before I had even landed I was turning to my left. The Idol was falling, but I was ready for it.

Unfortunately, it fell to my right.

Straight into the pocket of my father's dressing gown.

I had barely sat up when the door to the library burst open and in charged Feast the beast. Panic-stricken, I scurried backwards until I hit a bookshelf behind me. I was about to scream when Mrs Trot jumped over her counter and flicked a library card at my face.

'*Thief!*' she cried. '*I see you!*'

'And I see you,' I cried back at her. 'But that doesn't make me a thief. I'm the caretaker's new assistant. My name is Mr Weasel, but you can call me—'

'*Dare!*'

I looked beyond the snarling Feast just in time to see Miss Stickler march into the library. With a click of her fingers, the beast settled on the floor. 'It pains me to say it, Mrs Trot, but Hugo Dare isn't a thief,' Stickler sighed. 'No, he's something far worse than that.'

'But he came in through the skylight,' protested Trot. 'Are they not the actions of a thief?'

'Perhaps,' mused Stickler. 'Or maybe he was just cleaning the roof and fell in.'

'*That's it.*' I lifted the arm of my father's dressing gown and showed them the stains. 'Mr Bluff sent me up there and told me to make it sparkle,' I said.

'*Mr Bluff?*' Stickler turned on me in a flash. 'I thought Mr Bluff was on sick leave.'

'Not anymore, he isn't,' I said. 'He's in the Boiler Room. He's come back to work early.'

Stickler snorted loudly as she made her way towards the exit. 'I haven't got time for this nonsense,' she said. 'In ten minutes the doors will open and Coocamba's Idol will be on display for one hour and one hour only. Before that, however, there's somewhere I have to be ...'

With that, Miss Stickler hurried out of the library.

'Aren't you forgetting something, Weasel ... Dare ... whatever your name is?' scowled Trot, as I scrambled to my feet, ready to follow my Headteacher to safety. '*Something important?*'

'I don't need the toilet if that's what you mean,' I said.

'*Coocamba's Idol!*' Trot yelled. 'Put it back where you found it!'

I removed the carving from my dressing gown and placed it back on the plinth. 'I didn't find it ... *it found me.*'

'Same difference,' said Trot snottily.

I took one last look at her before I left and didn't like what I saw. For once it wasn't her face, though, that was causing me distress. No, it was the way she was holding her hand. 'Whatever you're about to do,' I said nervously, 'don't—'

'*Do it!*' Trot clicked her fingers. 'There,' she grinned. 'It's done.'

I was out the door before you could shout *he's behind you*. Ironically, that's exactly what Trot did shout, not that I needed reminding. Within seconds, Feast was hot on my heels, so much so, in fact, that if he'd been any closer he'd have been wearing my slippers. With the main body of the school in sight, I sped up and didn't look back until I finally passed through the double doors, stopping only to slam them behind me.

Why didn't I think of that before?

Yes, Feast was vicious. Yes, given the chance he would no doubt rip out my throat and chew on my tonsils. But what he didn't have was fingers. And without fingers he couldn't open the door.

The corridor was dark, but I pressed on regardless. I turned a corner and then another until the Boiler Room appeared in the distance. With any luck, Blind Man Bluff would be down there and I could warn him that Miss Stickler was on the warpath. Maybe he'd be so grateful he'd give me another sandwich in return. Or five. Or …

I was about to grab the handle when my foot tripped and I missed it completely. The last thing I saw before I hit the ground was the crutch. Not for the first time, it was the cause of my fall. Beside it, however, was something else. A body.

The body of Blind Man Bluff.

I looked again and realised my mistake.

No, it wasn't the body of Blind Man Bluff at all.

It was the *dead* body of Blind Man Bluff.

28.'IT'S A PINKY PROMISE FROM PINKY WEASEL.'

Or so I thought.

It's an easy mistake to make. Especially when the body was so *dead*-like.

With Blind Man Bluff slouched against the wall, I did the decent thing and lifted his head up by his nostrils so I could study his face. His eyes were closed, but he was still breathing. I looked a little closer and spotted a big red lump on his forehead. So, he wasn't dead and he wasn't asleep; he was unconscious. At a guess, he must've fallen and banged his head on the way down. Or maybe there was another explanation. His crutch was lying suspiciously by his side and the door to the Boiler Room was wide open.

Light-bulb moment.

I put two and two together and decided that Bluff must've been struck with his own crutch. Then I added another three and came to the conclusion that whoever had done it was somewhere down there in the bowels of the Boiler Room.

And that *whoever* was Wrinkles.

Maybe.

Surely Wrinkles would have used the knitting bag as her weapon of choice. And why bother hitting Bluff at all? He was hardly a threat. To himself perhaps, but that's not a good enough reason to knock him unconscious.

Whatever had happened, there was only one way to find out for sure. Picking the crutch up, I stepped over the caretaker and entered the Boiler Room. My last thought before I closed the door was one that had crossed my mind the last time I had been in this position.

Secrets of a Spy Number 42 – never walk knowingly into the unknown.

It wasn't the first time I had ignored my own advice.

I just hoped it wouldn't be the last.

My heart was punching a hole in my pyjamas as I took to the steps. According to Miss Stickler, Coocamba's Idol was on display for one hour starting from … *one minute ago.* Better set your stopwatch. If I'm still down here in fifty-nine minutes time, then I'll have failed. And that was something I couldn't let happen. If Coocamba's Idol was stolen (along with the contents of the Bottle Bank and the diamonds from the Pearly Gates) then mine would surely be the shortest career in SICK history. Less than forty-eight hours and counting. I'd spent longer burping.

I reached the bottom step and looked around. There was no one there. It was all clear. I mean, it wasn't as if there were lots of places to hide.

Except one.

Despite the heat, I crept forward and pressed my ear to the boiler. I listened hard, but heard nothing beyond a constant throbbing hum. Maybe I had been mistaken. Maybe the noises from before were just the grumblings of a boiler working tirelessly to heat the school.

'*Now what?*' My voice echoed around the room until, all of a sudden, it was drowned out by something much louder. The moaning and groaning had returned and whatever was doing it was trying hard to get my attention.

I dropped the crutch, took the biggest breath imaginable and squeezed down the gap between the boiler and the wall. I tried to ignore the heat, but the heat refused to ignore me. Before I knew it, I had started to sweat. When I did finally *know it*, I was dripping all over. I sucked in my stomach, flattened my face and carried on regardless. By the time I had reached the other side, I was completely drenched from head-to-slipper. More importantly, however, I had found what I was looking for.

There was a man behind the boiler.

A man who was even wetter than me.

A man who was even wetter than me despite wearing nothing but his underpants.

Silver Fox was on his knees with his forehead resting against the surface of the boiler. His eyes were closed and his mouth was covered by a strip of black tape. At least that explained the moaning and groaning.

Crouching down, I turned Fox's face towards me and flicked him three times on the nose to bring him back to reality.

'This might hurt a little,' I said. I considered peeling the tape off slowly, bit by bit. My other option, of course, was just to rip it off his mouth as quickly as possible.

I chose the other option.

'*Arrggghhh!*'

'I meant *a lot*,' I added hastily. 'As in, *this might hurt a lot*. Still, it's all over now. Count to ten and the pain will have passed. *One … two …*'

'*Three … four … five …*' Fox was nearly in tears as he worked his way through the numbers. '*Six … seven … the pain's worse than ever!*' he cried.

'Try and think about something else,' I said. 'Caterpillars perhaps. Or trampolines. Or—'

'*Stop!*' Fox tried to stand, but his hands had been bound together and chained to the boiler, preventing him from moving. 'There's no time for this,' he said. 'I've got an Idol to protect.'

'*We've* got an Idol to protect,' I said, correcting him. 'I am the caretaker's assistant, after all.'

'Oh, I should've guessed,' muttered Fox. 'Listen to me, Weasel. The same person who took off my clothes and chained me to this boiler is about to steal Coocamba's Idol.' As he spoke, the light in the Boiler Room began to flicker before it went out completely. 'That's her,' breathed Fox, clinging on to me in the darkness. 'I was worried she might come back … *and now she has!*'

'You wait here whilst I go and investigate,' I said, carefully removing Fox's fingers from my dressing gown.

'I've not got much choice, have I?' said Fox, rattling his

chains. 'You won't leave me, will you?'

'Of course not.' I held out my little finger as I finally slipped away. 'It's a pinky promise from Pinky Weasel.'

It was another hot encounter as I squeezed past the boiler. When I emerged out the other side, I set off across the room. I moved slowly at first with my arms outstretched, until my fingers brushed against the wall. I searched for the light switch and found it almost immediately. I gave it a flick and the Boiler Room was, once again, illuminated. That was easy.

Too easy.

I was about to head back to Silver Fox when I felt something hard poke me in the back of the head. It was an all too familiar feeling, although on this occasion I was fairly sure it wasn't Blind Man Bluff who was doing the poking. No, this time it was Wrinkles. She had chained Fox to the boiler and then dealt with Bluff, leaving the coast clear for her to steal Coocamba's Idol.

'I thought I told you not to interfere, Dare.'

Okay, so I was wrong. It wasn't Wrinkles.

It was Miss Stickler.

'Did Mr Bluff say you could borrow his crutch?' I asked.

'I don't need to ask permission.' Stickler poked me again to prove her point. 'Besides, he couldn't say much once I'd smashed him over the head with it!'

'You hit Blind Man Bluff?' I said, shocked. '*With his own crutch?* Was that really necessary?'

'Probably not,' admitted Stickler, 'but he shouldn't have come back to work so soon after his accident. I'm sure he regrets it now. As for you, Dare, stop talking and turn around slowly.'

'But that's two things at once,' I grumbled. 'One thing at once is hard enough. I've even been known to struggle when I'm doing absolutely nothing—'

'Just do it!' ordered Stickler.

So I did. Kind of. I half-shuffled around to face her with one hand over my mouth in case the odd word tried to sneak out.

'You're not funny,' said Stickler, moving my hand away with the crutch.

'I'm not trying to be,' I insisted. 'And I'm not trying to be rude either, but this is becoming extremely boring. You can't spend all day threatening me, Sticky. Not when there's a thief out there somewhere. They've already chained Mr Fox to the boiler and now they're going to steal Coocamba's Idol.'

'Yes, I am aware of that,' nodded Stickler.

'I even know who it is,' I blurted out.

'As do I,' said Stickler.

'And I can stop them,' I continued, 'but only if you'll let me ... *did you just say you know who the thief is?*'

'Of course.' Stickler began to laugh. A horrible girly giggle, it made my spine shiver. 'Isn't it obvious?' she said. 'It's you, Hugo Dare. You're the thief. *You're about to steal Coocamba's Idol!*'

29.'MELTED FOX.'

Wow! That was some curveball.

I hadn't seen it coming and yet I had been staring it straight in the face all this time. *It* being my good self. If Miss Stickler was right, then I, Hugo Dare, was the thief.

How come I had never realised?

Why had no one bothered to tell me?

And, perhaps more importantly, why hadn't I been caught yet?

Wait a second ...

It may have taken a moment or three, but my brain had finally surged into life.

No.

I didn't want to steal Coocamba's Idol.

And if I didn't want to, then I didn't have to.

That's how these things work, right?

Miss Stickler poked me again with the crutch. 'You're not really a caretaker's assistant, are you? You know far too much for that.'

'You've never said that before,' I replied. 'You used to tell me I had a mind like a loaf of bread.'

'That's true,' nodded Stickler, 'but now you're going to do something that a loaf of bread could never do. You're going to steal Coocamba's Idol. *Steal it for me!*'

'For you?' I laughed out loud as it finally dawned on me who the thief really was. 'Oh dear, Sticky, you're making a huge mistake,' I said. 'You're right. I'm not really a caretaker's assistant—'

'No, you're a minuscule speck of nothingness,' giggled Stickler, reaffirming herself as top *laugher* in the Boiler Room.

'That's where you're wrong,' I argued. 'I'm not a nothingness – I'm a *somethingness*. A *big* somethingness. And that big somethingness is a spy. I work for SICK. I'm SICK all over. SICK 'til the day I die.'

'Which hopefully won't be too far away,' smirked Stickler. 'I don't care what you think you are these days, Dare. All I need to remember is why I'm doing what I'm doing.'

'Which is *what?*' I shrugged. 'You're only trying to steal a wooden carving. It'd be easier just to buy one—'

'I don't want any old carving – *I want Coocamba's Idol!*' cried Stickler. 'It's worth more money than I can make in a lifetime. Enough for me to flee this horrible school and live out the rest of my days in luxury—'

Miss Stickler was stopped mid-sentence by the sound of groaning coming from behind the boiler. I knew what it was. Or rather who.

And, apparently, so did she.

'Poor Mr Fox,' said Stickler, feigning sadness. 'Like you, he works for SICK, but I only found out this morning when

I got an anonymous tip-off. That's why I had to deal with him the same way I dealt with Mr Bluff.'

'Did you take his clothes off as well?' I asked.

Stickler nodded. 'I had to. He wouldn't fit behind the boiler otherwise.'

'And you did?' I said in amazement.

Thankfully, Miss Stickler didn't hear me. 'Just imagine how hot he must be,' she said, running a hand over the surface of the boiler. 'It'd be even worse if I cranked up the temperature.'

I screwed up my face at the thought of it. 'Melted Fox.'

'Precisely,' said Stickler. 'And that's what will happen if you don't steal Coocamba's Idol for me. The temperature will increase and Mr Fox will be fried to a crisp—'

'Make your mind up!' I said. 'I thought we just agreed that he'd melt, not fry.'

'Either way he'll be dead,' said Stickler coldly. 'Do I need to spell it out any clearer?'

'You haven't spelt it out at all!' I said.

'Steal Coocamba's Idol and Fox lives,' Stickler spat. 'Don't ... *and he won't!* It's that simple. The clock is ticking, Dare. You've got forty-four minutes. After that the Idol will be gone for good—'

'*Bye.*' I didn't wait for Miss Stickler to finish her sentence. Talking took time and that was one thing I no longer had. If I was going to rescue Agent One then I had work to do. And it had nothing to do with being a caretaker's assistant.

For the first time in my life I was about to go against

everything I stood (and sat down) for.

I was going to steal Coocamba's Idol.

Charging out of the Boiler Room, I hopped over Blind Man Bluff and turned to my left.

Wrong way.

Bad start.

Spinning around, I set off again in the right direction. I used one eye to see where I was going whilst the other kept a look out for Feast as I hurried along the corridor. Thoughts peppered my brain as I ran. So Miss Stickler had intended to steal Coocamba's Idol all along. Or rather, she intended for *me* to steal it. Same difference I suppose. The only surprise was that I wasn't surprised. Her criminal tendencies seemed pretty much par for the course in Crooked Elbow. The Bottle Brothers and Detective Inspector Spite had pulled similar stunts, but on both those occasions someone had beaten them to it.

I just hoped that the same wrinkly someone would pay us a visit today. If only to prove me right.

It took me fifty-one seconds to get to the library. By the fifty-second I had decided to ignore both the drainpipe and the skylight and opted instead for the front entrance. Panting furiously, my breath steamed up the glass as I peered inside. If anything, I was expecting to see an impressive array of dignified guests, their eyes glued, naturally, to the far from magnificent wooden carving that was on display.

In actual fact, all hell had broken loose.

And, for once, it had nothing to do with me.

There was bedlam and bewilderment everywhere I

looked. Feast was howling at the ceiling, whilst Mrs Trot repeatedly scraped her teeth against her counter. The guests were either walking around in circles, their faces etched in horror, or crying in despair.

Then I saw the reason why.

Coocamba's Idol was missing from the top of the plinth.

It had already been stolen.

I ducked out of sight for fear of being spotted. Because being spotted meant being suspected. And being suspected meant being accused. And being accused meant going to prison. And going to prison meant cold showers, lumpy porridge and a huge, tattooed cellmate called Bruiser.

With that in mind, I stood back up again. If that was all prison could throw at me then it was a risk worth taking. If anything, I'd probably enjoy it.

Sneaking through the door, I took cover behind the first of twenty-six tall, free-standing bookcases that filled the library. The one that hid me included all the titles beginning with *A*. I waited a moment and then skipped quickly between bookcases. *A* to *E* without breaking stride for *B*, *C* and *D*. Aside from yours truly, there was only one other person who could cause such mayhem in a such small place in such a short space of time.

So where was she?

I spotted movement along the opposite aisle. Behind the *K* bookcase. *K* for *kaught* in the act.

It was Wrinkles.

She was on the move, her knitting bag clenched tightly in one hand as she shuffled slowly from *K* to *L* to *M* to *N* at a pace I hadn't seen since the first time we had met.

'Madam, I'm afraid you have to leave,' said Mrs Trot, as she appeared beside her. 'Not only is the library strictly out of bounds to members of the public, but the police are on their way to investigate a robbery.'

Without looking up, Wrinkles patted Mrs Trot gently on the head. That was when I spotted Coocamba's Idol. It was poking out the top of Wrinkles' knitting bag. *Why the cheek of it!* Not only had she managed to steal the Idol without anybody noticing, but now she was being actively encouraged to leave with it as well.

I had to do something.

Stepping out into the open, I lifted a finger and pointed it straight at Wrinkles. 'Stop right there, you wicked old worm!' I shouted.

Bad move, Hugo. Bad, bad move.

30.'THERE'S THE THIEF!'

You can turn as many pages as you like, but there's no getting away from it.

It was still a bad move.

And I was still a very silly spy.

'*There's the thief!*' screeched Mrs Trot, as she galloped towards me. 'He's already tried to steal the Idol once today ... *and now he's actually succeeded!*'

Trot stopped and clicked her fingers. Sure enough, Feast emerged from behind the counter. I held my ground, keen to see where he was heading. I was less keen when I realised he was heading straight for me.

Barring some kind of extraordinary miracle, I was about to be chewed up, spat out and then chewed up again for good measure.

Did I just write *extraordinary miracle?*

Because you're not going to believe this ...

I was all set for some skin-splitting, bone-biting agony when I noticed that the *A* bookcase had begun to topple forward. Like a row of giant dominoes, the effect spread quickly along the length of the library. *A* onto *B* onto *C* onto

D, bookcase after bookcase collided with the next one in line, sending books flying in every direction. Mrs Trot and the invited guests spotted the danger and dived for cover, powerless to stop the chaos from unfurling around them.

Sensing danger, Feast backed away, his fear of being squashed far greater than his need to take huge chunks out of yours truly. I, too, had the same fear as I ducked down behind the plinth. There was a shuddering *thud* as the *E* bookcase landed right on top of me. Somehow the plinth held firm and I remained, for the time being at least, far from pancake-like.

I looked around, but Wrinkles was nowhere to be seen. There was no doubt in my mind that she was to blame for the destruction of the library and now she had fled. I would've done much the same thing, but I couldn't. The front entrance was blocked by broken shelves from various bookcases which had crashed against the door, trapping all of us inside. Not only that, but my body was aching all over, my heart was beating fast and I had pigeon poop in my hair—

Whoa there, Hugo! Press the rewind button.

I brushed a hand over my head and examined what it left behind. Yes, I was right first time. But that wasn't possible. Not unless …

I looked up and saw that the skylight window was wide open with several feathery fiends hovering over the gap. It was a wonderful sight. I'm not ashamed to admit that I had never been so pleased to see a bird's bottom in all my life.

Crawling out from under the plinth, I climbed up onto

the fallen bookcase and reached for the opening. It wobbled a little, which didn't make things any easier. Then it wobbled a lot, which made them nigh on impossible. With nothing to lose, I leapt into the air, my fingers grasping desperately at the sides of the skylight. I took hold and then clung on the best I could. Finally I hauled myself up, careful not to snag my father's dressing gown as I passed through the window. Call me fussy, but I didn't want a rip in it so late in the book. Besides, you never know when a hole-free dressing gown might come in handy. And I don't just mean to hide my pyjamas.

I slammed the skylight shut and scampered towards the edge of the roof. With any luck, Wrinkles might still be on the school premises and I could spy her from my elevated position. The car park was clear, though, and there was nobody either coming or going through the gates. I spun around on the spot so I could scan the rest of the school grounds, but it was no use. It was a Wrinkles-free zone. She had gone.

Battered, bruised and beaten, I dropped my head and peered down at the ground below. Surely Wrinkles couldn't have escaped already. It wasn't possible.

I was right.

It wasn't possible.

To my amazement, Wrinkles was stood directly beneath me. With her back pressed against the library wall, I couldn't see her face, but I'd recognise that hood anywhere. If I jumped now I would probably land on top of her, squashing her into the concrete. Okay, so I'd probably end up with two broken legs in the process, but maybe it was a risk worth taking.

No, not maybe. *Definitely.*

I was about to make my move when Wrinkles glanced up. I held her stare as, for the first time, our eyes locked. I couldn't see mine, but hers were dark and deadly. Before I blinked, the hood fell from her head and I saw her properly for the first time. Her face didn't shock me – that was hideously grotesque as expected – but her hair did. It was brown in colour. Thick and luxurious.

I had seen that hair before.

Wrinkles pulled up her hood as she pushed herself off the wall. Slowly, she began to shuffle towards the school gates. She was leaving. And she was taking Coocamba's Idol with her.

I could've caught her up, but I didn't even try.

With just one look, everything had fallen into place. Chasing after Wrinkles was no longer my priority. Not anymore. Not now I knew where to find her. And find her I would. Of that I was certain.

All along I had suspected Wrinkles of being the thief and I was right. I had actually seen her with my own eyes on three separate occasions. She had stolen the contents of the Bottle Bank. She had filled her knitting bag with diamonds. And now she had taken Coocamba's Idol.

And yet that was only *half* true.

Wrinkles was just a curveball. She had been used to throw me off track and it had worked.

Almost.

Wrinkles *was* the thief, but there was somebody else. There had *always* been somebody else. Somebody who knew that the Bottle Brothers were going to rob their own bank. Somebody who knew that the Majestic Mob were smuggling diamonds into Crooked Elbow via the Pearly Gates Cemetery. And somebody who knew that Miss Stickler would try and steal Coocamba's Idol whilst it was being displayed at Crooked Comp'.

That *somebody* wasn't a mole passing top secret information to the enemy like the Big Cheese had suggested. They *were* the enemy. They were using the information for themselves.

And that same somebody knew that I, Hugo Dare, would eventually catch them out. They knew it and they didn't like it. Not one little bit. I'm not trying to blow my own balloon, but they feared me. They saw me as a threat.

And guess what? They were right to do so.

First things first, though, I had to get back to the SICK Bucket and tell the Big Cheese everything I knew. I needed him to believe me because if he didn't, well, then I would have to repeat myself until he did. Or until my tongue fell off, whichever came first. Although if my tongue fell off I could always write it down. Until my pen ran out. And then I'd get a pencil ...

Yes, convincing the Big Cheese was my priority, but that was the easy part. The hard part was getting off this roof.

Now, where did I leave that drainpipe?

31.'DON'T FORGET ABOUT ME!'

Now, I don't like to get ahead of myself (because once you leave yourself behind it's hard to catch up again), but aren't we forgetting someone?

Okay, aren't *I* forgetting someone?

As far as I was aware, Silver Fox was still in the Boiler Room, chained to the boiler, with the dastardly Miss Stickler for company. Life doesn't get much grimmer than that. To make matters worse, Stickler was also expecting me to return with Coocamba's Idol. That's the same Coocamba's Idol that had just been whisked away inside Wrinkles' knitting bag. The chances of me getting it back in the next few minutes were zero. The chances of me getting it back slightly later in the book, however, are much greater. Not that Stickler would wait that long.

Problem.

Fortunately, I had come up with a near perfect solution.

I could hear sirens in the distance as I scrambled down the drainpipe and raced across the school grounds.

First stop, the canteen.

No, don't be like that. This has got nothing to do with

my belly. If you don't believe me then turn away and count to ten. You won't miss a thing, I promise. There's just something I need to do …

Mission complete, I left the canteen and hurried back towards the Boiler Room. Blind Man Bluff was still where I had left him, unconscious in the doorway, minus his crutch. I patted his head for good luck before entering the room itself. Skipping down the steps, I kept my eyes peeled for any sign of Miss Stickler. I couldn't see her, but I knew she was down there somewhere, waiting to pounce.

Sure enough, the moment I hopped off the bottom step I felt a familiar prod in the back of my head.

'Have you got it?' Stickler asked.

'It depends on what *it* is,' I replied. 'Fleas? Itchy armpits? An irritating mother with a love of garden gnomes?'

'Coocamba's Idol,' snarled Stickler.

'Of course,' I smiled. 'I was just trying to lighten the mood. You seem so tense these days—'

'Where is it?' demanded Stickler, rudely interrupting me.

'Where do you think?' Call me a curious conversationalist, but I've always enjoyed answering a question with a question.

'You do know this isn't a game, don't you?' hissed Stickler.

'Do I look like I'm playing?' I said.

'You either have it or you have not,' spat Stickler. 'Which is it?'

'Which would you prefer?' I said.

On this occasion, Miss Stickler didn't answer. Instead,

she swung the crutch and took me out at the ankles, sending me tumbling to the ground. Now that hurt. *A lot.* It certainly wasn't the sort of reaction I'd expect from my Headteacher. Even one who disliked me as much as Stickler.

'If I wanted I could drive this crutch right up your nose until it comes out of your ear,' she warned me.

'I'm not sure you could *drive* it anywhere,' I said. 'Although, if you stick it between your legs you could always use it as a broomstick.' I shivered as the look on Stickler's face changed from angry to downright ugly. 'Remember, if you kill me now you'll never get your hands on what I've stolen for you,' I added hastily.

Miss Stickler lowered the crutch and took a step back. Slowly, so not to alarm her, I stood up and slipped my hand into my father's dressing gown.

'I've a question for you, Sticky,' I said, as my fingers stumbled upon what I was searching for. 'Do you know what Coocamba's Idol looks like?'

'Of course I do,' frowned Stickler.

'That's a shame.' Removing my hand, I pressed what I was carrying up to Stickler's face and shook it from side to side.

'Stop doing that!' she cried. 'I can't … *that's not the Idol!*'

'Isn't it?' I stopped shaking the bone I had taken from the fridge in the canteen and, instead, brought it crashing down on Miss Stickler's head.

At least, that was what I had planned.

Stickler, however, saw it coming and blocked it with the crutch. It was enough to send the bone spinning out of my hand, leaving me open to any potential attack. I cowered as Stickler raised the crutch, stepped forward ... *and stood on the bone!*

Like a freak circus act, she rolled backwards and forwards before she finally lost her balance. There were only two ways this could end. She would either hit something or fall over.

Or, fingers crossed, she could always do a bit of both.

My wish came true as Stickler crashed head-first into the boiler before collapsing to the ground. I waited for her to get up, but she never did. Crouching down, I lifted her wrist and checked her pulse. She had one. She was still alive. Which was good (for her at least, if nobody else).

'*Don't forget about me!*'

It was funny Silver Fox should say that because I had. Not to mention the bolt cutters I needed to free him from behind the boiler.

'Are you there?' Fox called out. 'Please ... I'm so hot my eyeballs are starting to sweat ...'

Hmm, that didn't sound good. And what I was about to tell him would hardly be music to his ears either.

'There's no easy way to say this,' I mumbled, '*so I won't bother!* See you later, Agent One.'

'You can't just leave me!' pleaded Fox.

'You're right,' I said, tiptoeing towards the steps. 'I can't ... and I shouldn't ... *but that doesn't mean I won't!*'

'*No!*' cried Fox.

'There's no need to panic,' I said. 'The police will be here soon to arrest Miss Stickler ... once I've called them. Ask nicely and I'm sure they'll free you.'

I was about to say goodbye, but decided against it. The sound of Silver Fox's desperate screams would only have drowned me out anyway. Instead, I covered my ears and dashed up the steps before I could get too emotional. It's never nice to hear a grown man cry. Unfortunately for Fox, though, not to mention the still comatose Blind Man Bluff, I had more pressing matters to attend to.

Wrinkles *and* the thief were in my sights.

Now all I had to do was make sure that the Big Cheese was looking in the same direction.

32.'THE ONLY TRUTH THAT MATTERS.'

It was early evening by the time I arrived at The Impossible Pizza.

Barring the odd speeding car and stumbling drunk, the streets of Crooked Elbow were largely deserted. I wasn't surprised. Given the choice, people preferred not to step out after dark if they could help it.

Unfortunately for me, I *couldn't* help it.

Not that I'm complaining, of course. If anything, I felt safer on my own. Being a spy, I can easily melt into my surroundings. I had nothing to fear.

I turned the doorknob three times to my left and twice to my right, trapping a finger in the process (so much for having nothing to fear). The Impossible Pizza was dark from ceiling to floor, but that didn't stop me from pressing on regardless. As I leant over the counter, I half-expected Impossible Rita to pop up in front of me. For once, I'd be pleased to see her.

And yet, for once, she never appeared.

I pressed the button and waited for the building to start shuddering. Maybe it was a spy's sixth sense, but my caution radar was at red alert. *Beware, Hugo Dare.* Because whatever *right* felt like, this wasn't it. Of that I was certain.

I climbed inside the rubbish chute and let go. Hurtling downwards, I barely noticed as my stomach began to turn somersaults. Three in total and then a double cartwheel as a grand finale. Impressive even by my standards. I readied myself for a soft landing as I neared the end, but my *human cuddle* was missing in action. Rumble, just like Impossible Rita, was nowhere to be seen.

My heart was beating like a champion egg whisker as I scraped myself up off the floor. Despite the darkness, I hurried across the SICK Bucket, swerving only once to avoid Miss Finefellow's desk. Her *empty* desk.

I was all set to charge into the Pantry when something held me back. Instead, I stopped, knocked and waited.

Nothing.

I stepped away from the door and took a moment to consider my next move. I knew what I *wanted* to do, but hiding in my shedroom until all this had blown over wasn't really an option. No, I was in too deep for that. Any deeper and I'd be drowning in SICK.

My mind shifted and I thought of the one person who could spur me on without even saying a word.

My father. *Dirk Dare.* The greatest spy who never was.

In the past few days I had become everything he had ever dreamt of. And that was why I couldn't let him down. Not now. Not when it mattered most.

I turned the handle and the door to the Pantry opened. I can't tell you what I had been expecting to find when I entered, but I *can* tell you what I *hadn't* been expecting and that was the Big Cheese laid flat-out across his writing table, laughing uncontrollably as he stared up at the ceiling.

Stood by his side was Miss Finefellow. She had a pad of paper in one hand and a pen in the other. I guessed she was taking notes, although I'm not entirely sure what notes you can take from the mouth of a giggling walrus.

'Ah, young Hare (*hiccup*).' The Big Cheese tried to sit up, but failed tragically. 'I wondered when you might come crawling back into my life,' he spluttered. 'Still in one piece, though. That's a loke of struck. Or is it a stroke of luck? Either way, am I right in thinking that everything went to plan (*hiccup*)?'

'Yes, it went to plan,' I nodded. 'Just not *my* plan.' I watched as the Big Cheese began to draw imaginary pictures in the air with his forefinger. 'Are you okay, sir? It's just … you don't really seem yourself.'

'And in what way, young Hare, am I not yourself (*hiccup*)?' mumbled the Big Cheese.

'You seem oddly cheerful,' I explained. 'And you keep hiccupping. And you've just called me by the wrong name. *Twice.*'

'I'll have you know that I am neither here nor there (*hiccup*), but somewhere in between,' remarked the Big Cheese bizarrely. With that, he rolled off the writing table straight into his armchair. Now I had a better view of him I knew for certain that something was wrong. Not only had his eyes glazed over, but he was also frothing at the mouth.

'*Pizza?*' said the Big Cheese, as he flattened a slice against his own forehead.

'Not today, sir.' Things must have been serious for me to turn down food. 'I'd rather just tell you what I know.'

'*What you know?*' Miss Finefellow snorted like a pig at feeding time. 'That shouldn't take long. Nevertheless, we are rather busy today, Dare. Have you got an appointment?'

'No, but *you* have,' I said. 'An appointment with the truth.'

'And what truth would that be?' smirked Finefellow.

'The only truth that matters,' I replied. 'The truth about the Bottle Bank. And the Pearly Gates Cemetery. And Crooked Comp'. And, most important of all, the truth about Wrinkles.'

'That's a whole lot of teeth ... tooth ... *truth*,' said the Big Cheese between mouthfuls. 'Right, let's hear it, shall we? *Wait!* Limber up your writing hand, Felicity (*hiccup*). I want you to make a note of everything young Hare says.'

'Certainly, sir,' said a smiling Finefellow. The smile vanished when she turned back towards me. 'You don't mind if I stay, do you, Dare? I'd hate to intrude.'

'It's not up to me what you do,' I shrugged.

'That's right, it's not,' said Finefellow, twirling the pen around her fingertips. 'Go on then. This should be interesting. After all, we've never had a spy quite like you before. You're a human disaster, Dare. You're so incompetent I wouldn't even trust you to get dressed in the morning. *Oh, look. You haven't.*'

'Now, now, Felicity (*hiccup*),' said the Big Cheese,

waving a hand at his secretary. 'Let's hear what young Hare has to say before we consign him to the SICK scrapheap.'

'Young *Dare*, sir,' I said.

'Yes, him as well,' the Big Cheese nodded. 'Right, chop-chop (*hiccup*). We haven't got all day.'

I tightened my dressing gown and drew the deepest breath imaginable. This was it. Time to drop the bomb.

The truth bomb.

'I was wrong,' I said.

'I knew it,' cried Finefellow. 'You're no better than your useless lump of a father. He can't even make a decent cup of tea after all these years—'

'*Freeze, Finefellow!*' I shouted. 'Dirk Dare is the greatest spy who never was—'

'Or just the worst tea-boy that *is*,' Finefellow shot back.

'*Play nicely!*' the Big Cheese roared. 'This isn't a game though, young Hare. Do you, or do you not, know something of interest (*hiccup*)?'

'I do,' I said.

'*And this isn't our wedding day either!*' yelled the Big Cheese. 'Just tell me what you know (*hiccup*). And whatever you do, don't mention that wrinkly old walnut.'

'As you wish, sir,' I said. 'Besides, why would I mention Wrinkles when Wrinkles isn't even the thief!'

'*Wrinkles … isn't … the … thief?*' the Big Cheese repeated. 'Well, I've known that all along, but you've always insisted she was behind every crime ever committed (*hiccup*). So, if it isn't Wrinkles, then who is it? And why haven't you dragged them kicking and screaming into the SICK Bucket?'

'There's no need to drag anybody anywhere,' I said. 'They're here already.'

The Big Cheese looked around, confused. '*Here?*'

'That's right, sir,' I nodded. 'The thief is in the Pantry.'

33.'YOU'RE NOT GOING ANYWHERE!'

The Big Cheese lifted one of his huge, sausage-like fingers and jabbed it in my direction.

'Ah, you had us fooled all along, young Hare,' he boomed, his moustache quivering as he spoke. 'It was a brilliant plan for someone so crushingly stupid (*hiccup*), but now you've finally confessed—'

'*Confessed?* I blurted out. 'I haven't confessed to anything. And why would I? I'm not the thief. And even if I was, do you really think I'd be so *crushingly stupid* as to admit it to you now?'

'Yes … no … maybe … *of course not!* groaned the Big Cheese. 'But if it's not you, then who is it (*hiccup*)? *Me?* I can't recall doing anything remotely dishonest, but all this pizza can't be good for my long-term memory.'

'No, sir, it's not you,' I said. 'You're SICK through and through. You live and breathe SICK.'

'Very true (*hiccup*),' agreed the Big Cheese. 'So, if it's not me, and it's not you, then—'

'That just leaves one other person,' I said.

The Big Cheese followed my gaze as I turned towards his secretary. '*Miss Finefellow?*' he barked. 'Are you crazy, young Hare (*hiccup*)?'

'*Dare!*' I said. 'And quite possibly. But if you'll just let me explain …'

'Be my guest (*hiccup*),' urged the Big Cheese. 'Although that's not an invitation for you to come and stay at my house.'

'And neither would I wish to, sir,' I said. 'Now, I'm no expert on the ways of women,' I began, suddenly serious, 'but I believe that Miss Finefellow is neither fine nor a fellow. What she is, however, is a thief. It was Finefellow who stole top secret information stored within the SICK Bucket and then used it to stay one step ahead of us at all times. It was Finefellow who robbed the Bottle Bank. It was Finefellow who emptied the diamonds from the boot of Spite's car at the Pearly Gates. And it was Finefellow who stole Coocamba's Idol. And she did it all disguised as Wrinkles.'

'How do you know this (*hiccup*)?' asked the Big Cheese.

'I don't,' I had to admit. 'Not really. Most of it's just guesswork with the odd nugget of truth thrown in for good measure. Like the fact I saw Miss Finefellow's hair at Crooked Comp' when Wrinkles' hood fell down. *And that she stinks so much!*'

'Bit rude,' said the Big Cheese, glancing awkwardly at his secretary.

'Of perfume,' I revealed. 'She uses it by the gallon-load to cover up the smell of rubber from Wrinkles' mask. And then there's the resignation letter I saw her writing this morning. You might not be aware of this, sir, but Finefellow doesn't need to work for SICK anymore. Not after everything she's stolen. Which also explains the holiday brochures she's been reading recently.' I turned to Miss Finefellow. 'It also explains why you pretend to hate me so much.'

'I'm not pretending,' said Finefellow coldly.

'That's what they all say,' I argued. 'No, you see me as a threat ... *and you're right to do so*. You knew it wouldn't be long before I discovered your little secret and that's why you've been telling the Big Cheese what a useless spy I am. He may have fallen for your lies, Finefellow, but I certainly haven't. You see, I always knew I was better than you said. And so did you.' I paused for breath. All this boasting was making me feel a little light-headed. 'So, tell me,' I said eventually, 'am I right ... *or am I right?*'

'Yes, don't keep us in suspenders, Felicity (*hiccup*),' pressed the Big Cheese. 'Is he right, left, or somewhere else entirely?'

Miss Finefellow threw her notepad down on the table and slowly parted her lips. 'Ten ... nine ... eight ...'

'What are you doing?' frowned the Big Cheese.

'Counting,' replied Finefellow matter-of-factly. 'Seven ... six ... five ...'

'Why?' I asked.

'Four ... you'll see,' said Finefellow. 'Three ... two ... one ... *and relax*.'

Right on cue, the Big Cheese tumbled out of his armchair

and collapsed face-first onto the carpet.

'*He's dead!*' I said, stunned. 'You just killed the Chief of SICK!'

'Don't be so over-dramatic!' scowled Finefellow. 'It's just a few sleeping pills in his pizza. Okay, a *lot* of sleeping pills, but that's his own fault for being such a stubborn old sloth. If you haven't already guessed, Dare, that's why he's been frothing at the mouth whilst hiccupping and talking absolute nonsense. Still, I knew he couldn't hold out forever. Unfortunately for the pair of you, he won't remember any of this when he wakes up. That'll be in about five hours' time. And, by then, I'll be long gone.'

'You're not the only one,' I muttered, glancing over my shoulder. The door was close. Close enough for me to kiss. On second thoughts, maybe I could just open it with my hand like a normal person. 'Right, this has been nice,' I said, shuffling backwards, 'but I've got things to do … people to see … mainly the Crooked Constabulary—'

'*You're not going anywhere!*'

With that, Miss Finefellow grabbed at an empty pizza box and flung it across the Pantry. It didn't have far to travel as it sliced through the air, before slicing through me a split-second later. I put my hands up to my face as blood began to gush from a cut just above my eye. It rolled down my cheek and onto my chin. Then it dripped.

'*You've done it now!*' I cried. '*There's blood on my father's dressing gown!*'

'Oh, I do hope that Crooked Elbow's number one tea-boy won't be too upset,' grinned Finefellow.

That was about as much as I could take. Fists raised, I rushed forward, only too aware that if I got close enough Finefellow wouldn't be able to do much damage with another pizza box. As it turns out, she didn't need to. Before I had a chance to squeeze her into a headlock, she reached inside her skirt and pulled out a knitting needle. I stopped when I felt it press against my Adam's Apple. Or, in this case, Hugo's Apple (as in the lump in my throat. Not any kind of fruit I just happened to be carrying around with me.)

'Like a good girl guide, I always come prepared,' grinned Finefellow, holding the needle still. 'You never know when things might get a little … *hairy*.'

'Or even *Dare-y*,' I said, too afraid to move. 'So, what are you going to do now? *Stab me?*'

'And get my needle dirty?' laughed Finefellow. 'I don't think so, do you? No, I've got a far better idea than that.' Moving the needle away from my throat, she gestured towards the door. 'Shall we go for a walk? And don't try anything silly, Dare. I'm stronger than you, quicker than you and, perhaps most important of all, smarter than you. Do as I say and you'll live a little longer.'

'How much longer?' I opened the door and walked out of the Pantry. '*Sixty … seventy … eighty years?*'

'I was thinking ten minutes,' said Finefellow. She followed close behind, the needle piercing my dressing gown as she poked me in the small of my back. 'Although I am prepared to stretch it to eleven. That way …' She pointed to her left and I spotted something that I never knew existed in the SICK Bucket.

A lift.

Finefellow pushed me inside and used the knitting needle to press *R* on the control panel.

'This is cosy,' I said, trying to lighten the mood as the door slid across and the lift jerked into life. 'Where are we going?'

'To the top,' revealed Finefellow. 'Don't get used to it, though. You'll soon be heading back down to the bottom.'

'That's a comforting thought,' I sighed. The lift pinged, the door opened and Miss Finefellow prodded me with the knitting needle. We were outside, three storeys up on the roof of The Impossible Pizza.

'Move,' demanded Finefellow.

'I think I've forgotten how to,' I said. 'Just give me a moment and I'll try to remember.'

Finefellow kicked the back of my legs, sending me stumbling forward. 'You're not funny, Dare,' she hissed. 'Tell me, why is it that you don't seem particularly scared?'

'The same reason you don't,' I said, wandering slowly across the roof.

'*Why would I be scared?*' laughed Finefellow. 'I'm not the one who's left a note downstairs in the Big Cheese's Pantry confessing to all those crimes.'

'Neither am I,' I said, confused.

'Oh, I think you'll find you are,' revealed Finefellow. 'I should know because it was me who wrote it for you. And now you're going to jump off the roof. That way the Big Cheese will wake up and think that you were the thief all along and I'll be free to spend my newly acquired wealth.

215

What do you think of that?'

'It's the worst plan I've ever heard,' I shrugged. 'But then I'm probably the wrong person to ask.'

I came to a halt at the edge of the roof. There was nowhere else to go.

'What are you waiting for, you revolting specimen? *Jump!*' said Finefellow impatiently.

And that, dear reader, is where my story first began. All those pages ago. In the prologue.

It was where we were first introduced.

And, if I'm not careful, it'll be where we sadly depart.

Now, where was I? Oh, yes …

Miss Finefellow prodded, the knitting needle stabbed and my body jerked. I began to wobble. Then I did something else entirely.

I fell off the roof.

'Goodbye,' said Finefellow. '*Forever.*'

This time there was no coming back. I was on my way. Over and out.

Going … going … gone.

34.'DEAD SIMPLE.'

Miss Finefellow turned and walked back along the length of the roof towards the lift.

She didn't wait for me to hit the ground.

And why would she?

She had seen it with her own eyes. My foot had slipped and I had wobbled back and forth until the fatal moment. I had tried – and failed – to save myself.

Hugo Dare – also known as Pink Weasel – *also* also known as Agent Minus Thirty-Five – was sadly no more.

Except that's not strictly true.

I had fallen, but I had done it deliberately. It's called jumping. You may be aware of it.

Secrets of a Spy Number 18 – always expect the unexpected even if the unexpected isn't that unexpected because you've been expecting it for some time.

It's probably too late to bring this up now, but have you never wondered why I've been wearing my father's dressing gown for the entire book? Did you just think it was me, Hugo Dare, toilet boy-turned-super spy, being ever so slightly weird?

Well, if that's the case then you'd be wrong. And you should also pay more attention. I've told you time and time again that my father, Dirk Dare, is the greatest spy who never was. Why would I say that if it wasn't true? Anyone would think he's done nothing for the past twenty-one years except make cups of tea in the SICK Bucket.

Which he has.

Mostly.

But when he wasn't drowning teabags in boiling water there was nothing he liked more than creating the secrets of a spy. Those very same secrets, in fact, that I've been quoting at regular intervals throughout this book.

There was one secret, however, that my father kept on returning to again and again. His own personal favourite.

Secrets of a Spy Number 1 – every great spy needs even greater gadgets.

Now, that's all well and good, but Dirk Dare isn't a spy and the Big Cheese doesn't do gadgets. That didn't stop my father, though. Determined as ever, he did what anybody else would do if they had the ways and means to do it.

He invented them himself.

See, not only is my father the greatest spy who never was, he's also a genius.

At least, that was what he had told me. Everyday. For as long as I can remember.

It was only now, as I jumped off the roof and began to plummet towards the pavement, that I started to wonder if he had been entirely truthful.

There's a space at the very top of thirteen Everyday

Avenue that most people would call the attic. My father, however, calls it his Inner Sanctum. It was here that he set to work. From the outside, it was hard to tell what was actually going on in there. From the inside, it was even harder. It was so cluttered that you could easily lose yourself. And I had. Three times, in fact. The mess didn't bother my father, though. He had invented things in there that would make your brain melt.

Shrinking trousers.

Edible satellites.

Toxic jelly babies.

Exploding coat hangers.

You can do a lot in twenty-one years if you put your mind to it. And my father *had* put his mind to it. *And what a bizarre mind it was!*

Then, three weeks ago, he called me up so he could show me his greatest achievement yet. It was a prototype for a set of *human* wings. Still untested, the idea behind them was that any man, woman or child would be able to soar through the air like a fully clothed bird with the aid of his invention. What he was most proud of, though, was the fact you could attach them to any piece of clothing and then conceal them completely until the time came when you needed to use them.

My father, ever the eccentric, fitted them to his dressing gown.

And the rest, as they say, is history. Or is it geography? Or is it just really, really obvious?

I had *borrowed* the dressing gown in case something like

this happened. And it had. Which made *right now* the most important moment of my life. The moment when I got to find out if the wings actually worked. Because if they didn't, and my father wasn't even half the genius he claimed he was, then I was about to see first-hand what my brains looked like splattered on the pavement. Except I wouldn't, of course. Because by then my eyeballs would almost certainly have popped out of their sockets and disappeared down the nearest drain.

Still, let's not dwell on the gory stuff ...

The first thing I did when I jumped off the roof was frantically flap my arms as if my life depended on it. It wasn't a good start. The wings popped out of my sleeves, but I was still falling fast. Nothing had changed.

I stopped flapping, stretched out my arms and let the wind blow under the wings. Suddenly my whole body jerked as if I was attached to a bungee rope. Yes, I was still falling, but now I was doing it at a much slower pace. Almost swooping down to the ground.

Almost ... whisper it ... *flying*.

I pulled up my legs ready for the moment of impact. With the wings working their magic, my landing was going to be less of a *splat* and more of a *thud*. Chipped toenails as opposed to broken bones.

Brace yourself, Hugo ...

I bounced three times as I hit the pavement, but somehow stayed on my feet. By the time I had skidded to a halt, The Impossible Pizza was some way behind me and the soles of my slippers were no more. I quickly tucked the wings into my father's dressing gown and turned back the way I had just come. To my surprise, Miss Finefellow was hurrying towards me with her head down. As far as I could tell, I had seen her, but she hadn't seen me.

'*Wrinkles!*'

Now she had.

'That's … not … possible,' muttered Finefellow, barely able to believe her own eyes. 'Still, I won't ask you how you did it … *because you won't be alive long enough to tell me!*'

Without breaking stride, Finefellow reached down and took off her high heels. I had no idea what she was doing. Come to think of it, I had no idea what I was doing. Or how I was going to do it when I finally figured it out.

Taking aim, Finefellow flicked her wrist and let fly with one of the heels. I didn't see its journey, but I felt its arrival as it struck me hard on the shoulder. I stumbled slightly, but it wasn't enough to stop me.

Unfortunately, the high heels came in a pair.

The second shoe hit me straight between the legs. Dropping to the ground, I curled up into a tiny ball and tried to shout, scream and even squeal but nothing came out. It was the same when I opened my mouth.

Somewhere in the distance, there was a howl of burning rubber as a car spun around the corner. I shielded my eyes, but the glare from its headlights still blinded me as it came racing up behind Finefellow.

'I don't mean to put a dampener on things, but I'm starting to think you're not the girl for me,' I moaned.

'About time,' smirked Finefellow. To my despair, she

was armed with another weapon. The knitting needle.

With an awkward clump, the car swerved off the road and mounted the pavement.

I looked again and realised it wasn't a car at all.

It was a milk float.

The knitting needle sparkled against the streetlamps as Finefellow lifted it above her head. 'For fear of repeating myself,' she began, none the wiser as to what was going on behind her, 'farewell, Hugo Dare ... *forever.*'

Scrambling up off the pavement, I did the sensible thing and dived head-first into a huge mound of black rubbish bags that had been piled up by the roadside. My landing was soft yet unpleasant. One hand buried itself deep into the remains of a takeaway kebab, whilst the other pressed down on a bulging nappy. That was nothing, however, compared to where my face ended up. I knew it was cat sick by the way it tasted. Still, I'm not fussy when it comes to food ...

I heard a screech of brakes, followed by an even louder screech from Finefellow.

And then ... *silence.*

I lay there for a moment before deciding it was safe to take a look. The milk float was only a whisker away from my slippers. Not one of my whiskers, of course. I haven't grown any yet. Nevertheless, it was still a whisker away and I was one extremely lucky spy.

Unlike Miss Finefellow.

She was laid flat-out on the pavement, slap-bang in the middle of an ever-expanding puddle of milk. There were smashed bottles all around her, not to mention the occasional crushed yogurt pot. It was a dairy disaster alright, but it still left me feeling like the cat that had got the cream.

I was about to crawl out of the rubbish bags when a man hopped down from the milk float.

A man ... but not a milkman.

'The evening is good, yes, Ugo Dayer,' said Murder. Curiously, he seemed even smaller than the last time I had seen him at the Bulging Bellyful. Smaller and chubbier. Not that it made him any less dangerous.

'Yes, I'm having a lovely evening,' I moaned. 'It's not often you get to leap from a three-storey building and then dine out on cat sick.'

Murder didn't reply. Instead, he shuffled over to Miss Finefellow and prodded her with his foot. She didn't move.

'Is she ... *you know?*' I asked.

'Is she *what?*' shrugged Murder. 'Is she covered in the milk? Is she wearing nothing on the feet? Is she—'

'*Dead?*' I blurted out.

Murder shook his balaclava. 'No, she is very much alive,' he said. 'That was my choice. If I wanted her to be dead, then dead she would be. It is that simple, no?'

'*Dead* simple,' I muttered. I looked on nervously as Murder stepped over Finefellow's body. He was coming for me and I had nothing to fight him off with. Only my fists and feet and they felt as if they belonged to someone else's body. 'I don't mean to sound ungrateful,' I began, 'but can't we rearrange this for another day. Next week perhaps. When I'm feeling a bit more like myself.'

Murder stopped walking. '*Next week?*' he repeated. 'No,

I is busy next week. But tomorrow ...' That was his cue to turn back towards the milk float. Climbing inside, he started the engine. 'One last thing,' he called out. 'The congratulations appear to be yours, Ugo Dayer. You have caught your thief, have you not?'

I watched as Murder reversed off the pavement and onto the road. It wasn't until the milk float had disappeared from view that I wandered over to where Miss Finefellow was laid out. Her chest was gently rising. Murder had been telling the truth; he hadn't killed her. Which was a relief, I suppose, as a dead body would take a lot of explaining. Instead, all I had to do was wake the Big Cheese and then contact the police before she came to. Then it would all be over.

As strange as it seemed, Murder was right.

The congratulations were all mine.

I, Hugo Dare, had caught the thief.

35.'THANKS FOR THE WARNING.'

Nine hours later I was sat on a wooden bench, surrounded by trees and grass, in the middle of Crooked Green.

I was all alone, but not through choice. My companion was late. Unacceptable behaviour really, especially seeing as it was his idea to meet at six o' clock in the morning. I was dark and cold and the night had barely slept a wink. Or something like that. Not to worry. I always rise early and, despite the wintry snap in the air, I still had my father's trusty dressing gown on to keep me nice and toasty.

My nostrils twitched as I spotted movement ahead of me. It took a while for me to make sense of what I was seeing, but I finally decided it was a rather large man in a lime green tracksuit, purple headband and bright orange trainers. He was running towards me. No, not running. *Waddling*. Like an over-fed duck wrapped in a rainbow.

Even from a distance I knew it was the Big Cheese. It was the moustache that gave him away. I'd recognise it anywhere, even in the bushy surroundings of Crooked Green.

'I've ... started ... jogging.' The bench strained under

the Big Cheese's weight as he sat down beside me. 'Yesterday was a wake-up call and I wasn't even napping,' he said. 'I let Miss Finefellow get the better of me and that will never do. The pizza got the better of me, too, although three or four slices from time to time can't be that bad, can it?'

'Probably not, sir,' I said, 'but three or four *boxes* every day is a different matter altogether.'

I wasn't trying to be funny, but that didn't stop the Big Cheese from starting to laugh.

'Ah, very good, young Dare,' he said, patting me on the back of my head with such ferocity that my teeth almost escaped from my gums. 'For someone with a brain like a damp towel, you've exceeded yourself these past few days. You told me we had a mole and then practically caught Miss Finefellow singlehandedly. It meant we could recover the contents from the vault in the Bottle Bank, the diamonds from the Pearly Gates and Coocamba's Idol. Most important of all though, you proved me wrong. That's as good as it gets, young Dare. Now, what did you want to see me about?'

I shook my head. 'I didn't, sir. You wanted to see me.'

'*Did I?*' The Big Cheese pulled on his moustache. 'I probably just wanted to check that you were still alive. Which you are. Bravo. Now, if that's all then I'd better be on my—'

'*Wait!*' There was a question I didn't want to ask, but couldn't really avoid. 'What happens to me now, sir? Do you want me to go back to the toilet?'

'*Back to the toilet?*' the Big Cheese barked. 'Not unless

you need to empty your bladder. No, from now on you're one of my spies, young Dare. You're Pink Weasel. Agent Minus Thirty-Five. I mean, you will have to go to school, of course, starting this morning. You are only thirteen, after all, and it's not as if Miss Stickler is there to turn you away at the gates. The rest of the time, however, you'll be working for me. I need you out on the streets, keeping the crooked out of Crooked Elbow.'

'And the Elbow, sir?' I said.

'The Elbow will have to stay, I'm afraid,' sighed the Big Cheese. 'Okay, enough of this idle chit-chat. Drop by the Pantry after school. There's something I need to run by you. Talking of which ...'

With that, the Big Cheese pushed himself up off the bench and waddled back the same way he had just come.

I waited a few minutes and then stood up myself, ready to follow the Chief of SICK out of Crooked Green. I hadn't eaten since Blind Man Bluff's delicious banana and pickle sandwiches the day before, but that was about to change.

I had a date.

A date with The Bulging Bellyful and one of their delicious Breakfast Surprises.

A sudden vibration in my armpit stopped me mid-dribble. Reaching inside my father's dressing gown, I pulled out my phone and studied the screen. *Unknown*. I should've guessed. There was still one loose thread, after all, I was yet to tie up.

'Ah, Murder – or should that be *Minkle Sparkes*,' I sniggered. 'I wondered when I was going to hear from you.'

'Then the time to wonder is no more,' said Murder. 'I is here and you is ... *in your shed, no?*'

I took a moment to answer. 'Yes, I'm in my shed,' I lied. 'Although I prefer to think of it as a shedroom. As in a shed-cum-bedroom. Mark my words, everybody will have one in a few years.'

'So, you is in your shedroom.' I heard a strange shuffling sound on the other end of the line. 'Yes, I can see you now,' Murder said eventually.

But how could he when I wasn't even there? Better than that, however, he had unknowingly given away his location.

I kept the phone pressed to my ear as I raced out of Crooked Green. The Bulging Bellyful would have to wait. Now I had a new destination in mind and, unlike the Big Cheese, I would have to run instead of waddle if I wanted to get there in time.

'Oh ... I forgot to ... thank you,' I said between breaths. With every step I was getting closer to home and, if my suspicions were correct, closer to Murder. 'For what you ... did yesterday ... outside ... The Impossible ... Pizza,' I panted. 'What I ... don't understand ... is why you ... did it?'

'I has my reasons,' said Murder.

'Which ... are?' I asked.

'None of your business,' said Murder bluntly. 'Now, be so kind and turn on the shedroom light.'

'*The shedroom ... light?*' I stopped running as I reached the entrance to Everyday Avenue. It was still dark and almost every house had its curtains closed. All except one, of course. 'I can't,' I said, as I slowly made my way towards number fourteen. 'The bulb's gone. And when I say gone, I mean it's vanished. As well as the light switch. Somebody's stolen them both. Was it you?'

'I do not steal the bulbs or the switches,' Murder growled. 'I steal souls. I is about to steal your soul.'

I leapt over the hedge and kept low as I crept across the Simples' front garden. I could see the outline of Murder as I peered up at the window. His rifle was balanced on the ledge. It was aiming straight at my shedroom.

'I don't see much use for souls,' I said quietly. At the same time I pressed down on the door handle. 'They're a bit like belly button fluff. Completely pointless.'

The door opened and I slipped inside.

'Why is you whispering?' asked Murder, as I moved carefully through the house.

'I'm ... *still asleep.*' I reached the staircase and put my foot on the bottom step. I waited for the inevitable creak, but it never came. 'I'm in bed and I'm trying not to wake myself,' I said.

'You should never have told me that,' laughed Murder. 'Your pillow is in my sights now. I suggest you move your head before I put the bullet in it.'

'Thanks for the warning.' I stopped at the top of the staircase. The door to my left was ajar. I could see flowery wallpaper and a beige carpet. And Murder. He was stood on a fluffy rug with his back to me. The window was open and he was leaning out of it. Preparing himself for the shot.

'It has been knowing you nice,' said Murder, as he took aim. 'Sleep tight, Ugo Dayer ...'

I flinched as he fired two shots. Then I made my move.

'Nice try,' I said, creeping up behind him, 'but you should really have looked a little closer to home!'

Murder swung the rifle in my direction. Before he could fire, I crouched down and grabbed the rug from under his feet. I gave it a sharp tug and Murder stumbled backwards. To my surprise, he let go of the rifle and it flew out of the window. To my *double* surprise, Murder followed it a moment later. I rushed forward to see what had happened, half-expecting to find him laid out across the front garden.

Wrong again, Hugo.

'*Help me!*' begged Murder, as he clung onto the window ledge with both hands. '*Please!*'

'Maybe, maybe not.' Yes, I know I couldn't just let him drop, but I wasn't about to drag him to safety either. Not until I knew who it was who had been terrorising me these past few days. 'Take off your balaclava,' I said.

Murder shook his head. 'Never.'

One by one, I began to tickle his fingers.

'*Don't do that!*' yelled Murder. 'I'll fall.'

'That's the idea,' I said. 'Take off your balaclava and I'll stop.'

'I've got a better idea.' Murder's voice had changed. Not only was he breathing hard, but his accent had disappeared. 'I'll take off my balaclava if you take off that dressing gown!' he said.

'I beg your pardon!' I said.

'I'm not joking!' cried Murder, struggling to hold himself up. 'I *need* that dressing gown!'

'So do I,' I said. 'It's not exactly tropical in here. Now take off your balaclava.'

Murder was weakening. I could see it in his eyes. One way or another, this was about to end.

'Okay, you win,' he said. 'But understand one thing, Hugo. Everything I've ever done has been for your benefit. Right, this might come as a bit of a shock ...'

Murder removed one hand from the window ledge and pulled off his balaclava. I blinked once in horror. Then twice more in disbelief. Then, as a last resort, I closed my eyes completely. When I opened them again, the same face was still there, staring back at me. It was round like a watermelon with rosy cheeks and eyebrows that met in the middle.

'*You!*' I gasped.

'Yes, me,' replied the man that up until a few seconds ago I had simply known as Murder. Now I knew differently. *Very* differently. As unlikely as it seemed, I knew this man better than anybody else in the whole of Crooked Elbow.

'*You!*' I said again.

'Yes, Hugo, I think we're both fully aware that I am, indeed, *me*,' groaned my father, as he gripped on for dear life. 'Now, be a good son and pass me my dressing gown ... *preferably before my arms drop off!*'

36.'IT'S WHAT I'VE ALWAYS DONE BEST.'

When I was young I always thought my father, Dirk Dare, could do anything.

I thought he was unstoppable. Invincible. A real-life superhero. Then, as I got older, I realised he really was. Most children's fathers did something boring for a living. They worked in banks and offices, sausage factories and sewerage farms. Mine worked for SICK. Okay, so he spent his days warming the teapot, but that was good enough for me. I was even more impressed when he said he could me get a job there. I was going to be a spy. Or a toilet boy. Either way, I was following in his footsteps.

My father. The man who would do anything for me.

Now call me ungrateful, but I don't think that *doing anything* should include repeatedly trying to kill me. That, by any stretch of even the *stretchiest* of imaginations, is at least one stretch too far.

'*You!*' In the end I decided to keep the dressing gown where it was and helped my father to climb back through the window instead. '*You!*'

'Yes, yes, Hugo, we've already done the introductions,' said Dirk, as his boots settled on the Simples' bedroom carpet. 'I am me and you are you ... how extraordinary ... blah, blah, blah. That was a close call, though,' he said, peering out of the window. 'Why did you pull that rug out from under my feet? Have you lost your marbles?'

'*You!*' I said again. 'You're ... *Murder!* You're ... *Minkle Sparkes!*'

'The one and only,' admitted Dirk. 'Well, not quite the one and only. There are lots of Minkle Sparkes as it happens. I'm surprised you didn't recognise the name. It's printed on all the teacups in the SICK Bucket. Minkle Sparkes make crockery.'

Of course they did. I knew the name rang a bell. Shame it wasn't loud enough for me to hear.

'We should probably get out of here before we're rumbled,' said Dirk, as he closed the curtains. 'We don't want anybody calling the police, do we? Or, worse than that, calling your mother. She'll wring my flabby neck if she finds out I've borrowed the Simples' key. Are you ready?'

'Not yet.' I sat down on the Simples' bed to prove my point. 'Not until you've told me why.'

'Why *what?*' shrugged Dirk.

'Why *everything,*' I said. 'Why you shattered my window and put bullet holes in my mattress? Why you stole a milk float, knocked me over and then almost crushed me with a crate of milk bottles? Why you broke into my shedroom before running away from the lawnmower? Why you tried to slice me up in The Bulging Bellyful with a knife and fork? Would you like me to go on?'

'If you like,' grinned Dirk.

'No, I *don't* like!' I stopped to think. 'I suppose you did help me with Finefellow. If it wasn't for you I would never have caught her.'

'No, if it wasn't for *you* you would never have caught her,' argued Dirk. 'I just gave her a nudge in the right direction. I am proud of my other achievements, though.'

'*Achievements?*' I cried. 'All you've done is try to kill me at every available opportunity. I'm lucky to still be alive. By the way, why *do* you hate me so much?'

'*Hate you?*' Dirk screwed up his face as he slung his rifle over his shoulder. 'I don't hate you. I don't even mildly dislike you. *Why would I?* You're the son I always wanted.'

'*Am I?*' I said, amazed.

'Of course you are,' said Dirk. 'I'm not trying to kill you, Hugo – I'm *training* you. I want you to become the finest spy on the planet. The best in the business. Most of all, I don't want you to end up like me. Your mother calls me a pork pie of a man and she's right. I've spent the past twenty-one years making cups of tea for people who are either too lazy or too stupid to make it themselves. You're better than that, though. You're the future of SICK. And I'm the proudest father in Crooked Elbow.'

'I think it's time we left.' I lowered my head and stared blindly at the beige carpet as I wandered out of the Simples' bedroom. I didn't want my father to see the tears that were rolling down my cheeks. Thankfully, he was too busy wiping his own to notice.

We didn't say another word as we left the house. We

were about to cross the road and go home when a car sped into Everyday Avenue. I tensed up, but then immediately relaxed when I saw that its bonnet was completely crushed.

'Good morning, Weasel,' said Silver Fox, as the hearse shuddered to a halt. '*Now get in!*'

'I would if I could, but I've got to go to school,' I said.

'School can wait – this can't,' insisted Fox. 'Crooked Elbow is on the brink of disaster so the Big Cheese needs his best agents on the case … *oh, and you as well!*' Fox was about to laugh at his own joke when he caught sight of my father. By the look on his face he didn't like what he saw. Admittedly, dressed all in black with a balaclava balanced on his head, Dirk Dare did bear more than a passing resemblance to your average burglar. 'Who's your friend?' Fox asked.

It made me sad to think that Agent One didn't recognise my father, especially after all those years he'd spent serving drinks in the SICK Bucket.

'He's not my friend,' I replied. 'He's my—'

'We've got to go,' said Fox, butting-in. 'In fact, if you don't get in this minute, the Big Cheese will see that to it that you're travelling in a hearse for all the wrong reasons. *Understand?*'

Unfortunately, I did. Hurrying around to the passenger side, I was all set to get in when a thought crossed my mind. My father looked lost, stood there on the pavement, all alone. Yes, a little like a pork pie perhaps, but this was one that had escaped from a shopping basket by accident and was now in danger of being trampled underfoot.

'Why don't you hop in?' I said, opening the door to the hearse. 'You've always wanted to see what spies get up to. This is your chance.'

Dirk tried to smile, but failed miserably. 'I don't think so, do you? No, my place is back home with your mother. I'll make her a nice cup of tea and all will be forgiven. It's what I do best, remember. It's what I've *always* done best.'

I was about to speak when Fox stamped down on the accelerator and the hearse shot forward. Without thinking, I jumped inside and strapped on my seat belt in case I got left behind. We had barely moved before Fox spun the steering wheel, performing a smart U-turn in the middle of Everyday Avenue. As we passed number fourteen I looked out for my father, but he was nowhere to be seen. I felt both a twinge of guilt and a tingle of sadness (an uncomfortable coupling if ever there was one) as I realised he had already gone back home. Back to my mother. Back to his Inner Sanctum and his inventions. Maybe my father, the greatest spy who never was, really was at his best making cups of tea for other people. He had, after all, spent a large chunk of his life doing it.

I, however, had no intention of taking over his teapot.

I was the spy who came in from the toilet.

Codename Pink Weasel.

Agent Minus Thirty-Five.

My time was now.

THE END

HUGO DARE WILL RETURN

IN…

THE WEASEL HAS LANDED

ACKNOWLEDGEMENTS

Thanks to the wonderful Sian Phillips for her eagle-eyed editing skills and glowing praise.

Thanks to the wonderful Stuart Bache and all the team at Books Covered for the front cover.

Thanks to everyone at the wonderful Polgarus Studio for their first-rate formatting.

Note to self – try to look for another word other than wonderful before anybody reads this. Do not forget. Because that would be really embarrassing. I'm embarrassed enough already just thinking about it.

AUTHOR FACTFILE

NAME: David Codd. But you can call me David Codd. Because that's my name. Obviously.

DATE OF BIRTH: Sometime in the past. It's all a little hazy. I'm not entirely convinced I was even there if I'm being honest.

BIRTHPLACE: In a hospital. In Lincoln. In Lincolnshire. In England.

ADDRESS: No, thank you. I don't like the feel of the wind against my bare legs.

HEIGHT: Taller than a squirrel but much shorter than a lamppost. Just somewhere in between.

WEIGHT: What for?

OCCUPATION: Writing this. It doesn't just happen by itself. Or maybe it does.

LIKES: Norwich City football club, running, desert boots, parsnips.

DISLIKES: Norwich City football club, running, rain, Brussels sprouts.

REASON FOR WRITING: I wanted to give my fingers some exercise. They were getting lazy, just hanging there, flapping about.

ANYTHING ELSE: Thank you for reading this book. If you've got this far then you deserve a medal. Just don't ask me for one. Because I haven't got any. But I am very grateful. And do feel free to leave a review on Amazon if leaving reviews on Amazon is your kind of thing. Until the next time …